SCORPION

A GOOD BAD HORSE

Scorpion

A GOOD BAD HORSE

by

WILL JAMES

Illustrated by the Author

UNIVERSITY OF NEBRASKA PRESS
Lincoln and London

Library of Congress Catalog Number 36–23527
International Standard Book Number 0–8032–5822–4

First Bison Book printing: 1975
Most recent printing shown by first digit below:
2 3 4 5 6 7 8 9 10

Bison Book edition published by arrangement with Charles Scribner's Sons.

Manufactured in the United States of America

ILLUSTRATIONS

ILLUSTRATIONS

SCORPION
A GOOD BAD HORSE

INTRODUCTION

HE wasn't a big horse, didn't weigh over a thousand pounds, and his narrow withers would hardly measure up to five feet. But that's just a guess, for no horse is ever measured in the cow country, not by size, only by what he's made of and what he might be good for.

Scorpion, as the cowboy who started to break him named him, was an average size range saddle horse, the right size for all around range work, for rough country and mountains and for fast outside roping or cutting out, and if a man sat him like a rider and not like a pack, he could go circles around the bigger horses any place or time. The riders who eased themselves in the saddle on his back didn't set him like packs, they sat him as riders should and when Scorpion unwound and they hit the ground they bowed to him as riders would, when they could. But Scorpion did pack a human pack, not a cowboy nor a top rider, and how that come about is where this story comes in.

CHAPTER ONE

THE first horse that would draw your eye amongst a corralful of other horses or outside in the hills would be Scorpion, and that wouldn't be on account of any bald face or spots on him, for he was of solid color, a deep chestnut sorrel, his head darker than his dappled body.

But even that pretty color wasn't what caught the eye, it was the contrast of his slim and graceful and bowed neck holding up a vicious looking and roman nosed head, all but for the eyes which showed no white and was as dark and docile looking as some old pet milk cow's.

The build of his wiry body matched the style of his neck, narrow but deep chested and long shoulders smoothing down to bulging forearms. The withers was high, the back was short to long sloping rounded hips which was narrower than the thighs and tapered to smooth muscles to the hocks. From hocks and knees the not too slim but fine legs tapered to not too long an ankle, and to undercap them was bluish gray, small rounded hoofs, the same color as some flint is and just as hard. Scorpion had been raised in rough and rocky country.

The horse round-up was once a year in that country,

in the summer, when the young colts would be branded and geldings from three years old on up would be kept at the ranch pasture to be broke to ride or work, also others to be shipped out and sold.

Scorpion was a well developed five year old when the cowboy, Pete Leon, dabbed his rope on him for the first time, and even tho Pete had rode the rough off hundreds of tough broncs and got so he hardly seemed to notice their wild and wicked actions, he showed new interest at the first roping and handling of this chestnut.

With the handling and riding of many different horses every day, day in and day out for many years, Pete had got so he could near tell at a glance what a bronc's nature was, how he would act and how much of a fight there'd be, and he'd treat the horse according. After the fourth or fifth saddling he would name the horse by some character of him, or marks on his hide, or by some happening while breaking him, and by that time he could near tell what that certain bronc would turn out to be after the final education with stock at round-ups, and he seldom made mistakes that way.

But the chestnut had fooled this cowboy from the start. Pete had glanced at him a little more than he had the other broncs, that was on account of the vicious looking roman nosed head on such a well built body in every way. The mild big brown eyes is what had fooled him, and he'd figured that the vicious looking shaped head was just a mistake of nature. The horse might turn out to be a little tougher than the average, a little

The first horse that would draw your eye amongst a corralful of other horses or outside in the hills would be Scorpion

harder to "bust" (stop and turn) and bring on a few new tricks, but all broncs acted more or less different anyway, and he didn't figure that this chestnut would be a much harder nut to set and crack than the average bronc, and not near as hard as some he'd took the rough off of, like some of them old experienced and spoiled outlaws.

The second Pete spread his loop and caught the chestnut by the forefeet is when that cowboy started doubting his quick judgment of that horse's nature. The chestnut hit the end of the rope like the good wild one he was, but he wasn't to be throwed so a hackamore could be slipped on his head while he was down. Instead, and by what seemed a miracle, he kept his feet, and after only a few tries at breaking loose he turned to face the cowboy.

Pete went along the rope then to get a shorter and better holt and jerk the front feet out from under him when he would scare and turn to try and get away. But the horse didn't scare much nor turn. He only sort of crouched and slid back on his front feet some and eyeing Pete steady as that cowboy came closer.

As he came still closer, Pete noticed something mighty queer about the look in that horse's eyes. He'd at first thought 'em docile looking and showing a heap kinder disposition than the shape of his head indicated. But now he seen there was a deep look in them eyes, mysterious and threatening like, and they didn't seem to look at the cowboy but on both sides of him, like he wasn't there.

Pete had broke two horses that had looked beyond him that way. He would always remember them, for they'd been killers. One had killed one man and badly hurt some others, and the other one had near killed two men before he was downed with a bullet. It seemed like them ponies had been born with murder in their hearts, and they'd pounced with teeth and hoofs when their victims couldn't very well get away. They would watch for such a chance, and Pete well remembered the narrow escapes and battles he'd had with 'em.

Now he shivered a little at the mysterious look in the chestnut's eyes. No fear in 'em, and that wasn't natural for range bred horses that run as free as deer and are corralled only once a year. But this chestnut had them big dark eyes. The killers' eyes had been little, sunken, and a lot of white showed around when excited and on the fight, and even tho there was the same look with him as with the two killers' eyes there was something else which was as beyond Pete to figure out as them eyes looked, beyond and one eye past each side of him.

Pete shrugged. There couldn't be no more such horses as the two killers he'd "started" a few years ago, he thought, and as he went still closer to the chestnut he felt a little foolish for spending so much time in trying to figure out one mean looking headed bronc. He'd handled a lot of mean ones. But none as queer and mysterious acting as this chestnut, not even the killers.

As he came closer the chestnut only straightened up on his spread legs, quivered, bowed his neck and only snorted low, still looking beyond and on both sides of

Pete. Pete was only about ten feet from the horse then, and a natural acting range bronc would of tore the earth to turn and try to get away, but the chestnut stood his ground and only quivered.

So, to get things started, Pete made a sudden run at him to scare him to turning fast enough so he could throw him and then put the hackamore on him. (It's never thought of to try to put a hackamore on a first caught bronc while he's standing, not unless he's in a chute.) But the chestnut didn't scare much. He turned, but too easy to get throwed, and then is when Pete got to thinking that the horse had been forefooted and throwed before, and maybe rode. But that couldn't be. The horse hadn't been missed at none of the round-ups since he was branded, when a young colt, and anybody starting breaking him would of sure finished the job, it looked like, then there was no saddle marks on his short back.

He would soon find out. Getting to within a few feet of the horse, Pete went to flip the end of a soft tie rope around his forefeet, figuring on hobbling him before he fought out of the loop that held 'em—and then's when the horse come to life, so sudden that Pete, with all his experience with striking broncs, was a little too close. Both hoofs came up, glanced on his shoulder and tore one side of his vest off along with the front of his shirt.

It all happened so quick that he hardly seen the horse move. But even if Pete did get a little careless his experience at handling mean horses sure saved him from real harm. Natural like from such experience, he kept the slack of his rope tight and the loop stayed on the horse's both forefeet. As the chestnut reared and fought at the rope, Pete took sudden advantage of that, and knowing that if the rope was kept tight a green bronc would often throw himself over backwards that way, he handled his rope to that effect.

The chestnut, straight up on his hind legs, pawed the air a few times with his forefeet. Then, like to get away from the rope he jerked back, and that was his undoing. In another second he lit hard to the ground.

But like a rubber ball he bounced up again, only too late, for Pete, working like lightning, keeping the rope tight and jerking it at the right time, kept the horse from getting his feet under him every time he'd lunge and bounce up. After many tries, the chestnut, finally out of breath, layed still. But it wouldn't be for long and Pete wasn't slow in taking advantage of that spell. He reached for the soft and heavy tie rope and in a few seconds had him tied down to stay.

And not any too soon, for the horse begin to struggle to get up again, and after a few mighty good tries layed still, breathing hard.

Pete hunted the remains of his vest for his tobacco, rolled a smoke and looking down at the chestnut he remarked, "That pony sure knows when there's any use of fighting and when there ain't."

After a while he slipped the hackamore on the horse's head, and wanting to test his temper, he got a small willow stick about the size of a thumb and placed it in the side of the horse's mouth. It was snapped off as tho it was a match.

"Hoomp," Pete grunted at him. "Good horse, but you'll sure need watching."

He slapped his rawhide hobbles on the chestnut's fore feet and then with the end of the long tie rope made a collar around his neck and untied his feet, keeping one left hind foot tied to the collar and leaving enough slack so that when the horse stood up that hind foot would be drawed forward so it'd barely touch the ground.

With such tying a horse can stand up but he's sure handicapped as to much action. He can't strike very well on account he needs his two hind legs to stand on to do that, and he can't kick back with the one hind leg on account of it being tied to the collar and so it barely touches the ground. But he can kick forward, and some can reach as far as their ears. A cowboy just has to watch out for that, and many other things.

The chestnut still laying and not knowing he could now stand, Pete slapped him on the neck with the flat of his hand and, after testing the ropes and hobbles well, he scrambled to his feet. He stood a while, quivering, and then tested the ropes and hobbles some more until he made sure they would hold, and when he stood again and faced Pete his eyes seemed to look still further past that cowboy, and they was still darker.

"There's no use of you getting that far away look and all het up," says the cowboy as he started after his saddle; "your work is going to be right here for a spell and you'd just as well take it cool."

The chestnut never batted an eye nor wiggled an ear, hardly even when the cowboy came back with his saddle and picked up the hackamore rope. It wasn't until the saddle was brought up to set on his back that he came out of his trancelike stand and went into action. He done that well. Even and tho handicapped as he was the saddle was near kicked out of Pete's hands by that tied hoof which couldn't kick back but could sure reach ahead near to where Pete had been standing, at the point of the horse's shoulder.

The saddle didn't get to rest on the chestnut's back until the third try, and then Pete had to hang onto it and hold it there until the horse got thru with another fit. (It spoils a horse quick to let him buck a saddle off at the first saddlings.) Another fit was brought on as the cinch was reached for and drawed up under his belly but the latigo was thru the cinch ring by then, and as Pete pulled on it the saddle was held in place until the horse quieted down.

Just taking the rough off broncs the way Pete was contracted to do for the Cross Bell outfit he didn't try to do any educating much. He just had to have the broncs gentled so they could be saddled without them having to be throwed and tied down, and take the buck and fight out of 'em as much as possible, not wear themselves out that way and so some work could be done with 'em. He didn't break 'em to lead first as is done with broncs that's to be turned over as broke, he just broke 'em from running on a rope when caught, broke 'em to stand with only hobbles while being saddled, and then there was about half an hour of riding each day, scaring the buck out of 'em with a flat and loud popping quirt (more noise than sting), then trot and lope 'em back and forth into a big square corral, turn 'em this way and that way, stop 'em and start 'em again, get off and get on, and after a couple of saddlings the horse is rode out in the open for more running, turning, and stopping.

Eight or ten saddlings usually takes the rough off an average bronc. That means eight or ten days for each, and bronc peelers on contract as Pete was, take from eight to ten broncs at a time, riding every one each day and used from half to an hour's time on each bronc. That's a good rough day's work.

Not much time was spent on the chestnut's first saddling, for as it is with all broncs when first caught, they're too scared or confused or mad and nothing can be teached 'em then only that they know they've been stopped by a rope, and that they've been saddled and rode.

The chestnut was both confused and mad, but not much scared with the first saddling, and when he fought it was more on account that all was so strange and his wanting to break away from what held him. The man he mistrusted more than feared, that was his natural instinct against humans, and to top that there was a confidence or feeling that he could best him, even if for the time the man did have him pretty well helpless. His eyes and ears always seemed to be aimed at far distances; however, he could always see that man's every move without cocking an ear or looking his direction.

Standing close to the horse's shoulder, Pete gathered his hackamore reins, wiggled his saddle a bit and then stuck his boot toe in the stirrup, all the while watching the horse's ears and eyes for an inkling as to what to expect. But no hint come from there, for the horse, if he seemed interested in any direction, that was straight ahead. Pete didn't like that, it sort of left him in the dark with plenty to stumble on. He pulled on the hackamore rein and got the horse's head close to him.

The chestnut was still acting kind of blank when, as Pete put weight in the stirrup to ease himself up a bit and towards getting into the saddle, that horse's tied hind hoof came up like fired out of a gun and kicked the stirrup off his foot.

A glance at the chestnut's ears in that same second showed that they was still pointing neutral. Pete's spur rowel was still ringing from the kick as he started pulling up his shap belt. He pulled his hat down tight and he mumbled words to the effect that there was no use fooling around.

He bent the horse's neck to a half circle and held his nose close to his left hip and stuck his toe in the stirrup once more, this time putting plenty of weight in it, and that brought plenty of sudden action.—The stirrup was kicked at once more, but missed this time, and things started from there.

Standing in one stirrup, one hand on the horn and the other with a close holt on the left hackamore rein, Pete done his riding there, not at all an easy thing to

Pete was still riding when the horse sort of upended in mid air

do but the wisest thing to try to do when a bronc's front feet are hobbled and a hind one tied up, for a horse will easy fall then when trying to buck, and maybe turn over a few times.

The chestnut was already wise enough as to what he could do without taking the chance of falling. He didn't want to fall, not unless he could get the rider under him by doing that, and as it was, with the way he was handicapped he done a pretty fair job of bucking. It was a wonder to Pete that he stood on his feet and he was expecting him to fold up and turn over at every jump, which came faster than the eye could see.

But all was going too well, for the chestnut, and getting sort of enthused he made one high popping leap, and Pete was still riding when the horse sort of upended in mid air and came down on his neck, dazing and near knocking the breath out of him.

He layed on his side for a few seconds, and Pete was standing by him when he raised his head. Another slap on the neck and the chestnut struggled up to his feet again. As he did the cowboy stuck his toe in the stirrup and as the horse came up he came up with him, and as he went to stand that cowboy had eased himself in the saddle this time.

That all was a little too much for the chestnut, and he just stood and quivered. That clinging rider and then that fall and now right in the middle of him, sort of showed that for the time that rider sure had won.

While all that was going on in that horse's think tank, Pete now begin climbing off and on him again, just to get the horse used to that and to show him there was no sense of fighting. He done that a few times while the horse never blinked an eye or moved a hoof, and then he took the foot rope and hobbles off.

The horse still stood, and Pete eased in the saddle again, letting him stand some more. Then he pulled on one rein, and the horse now knowing his feet was free didn't move, he just sort of exploded and sailed near as high as the corral he was in. But his leaving the earth was a harder jolt on Pete than the coming down, for the horse didn't land stiff and hard and crooked as in a buck jump but more like he'd went over a high hurdle and as tho he'd just wanted to shed clear of the shackles that'd been holding him. When he landed, fifteen feet away from where he left the earth at a stand still, he just crowhopped a couple of easy jumps, and to Pete's surprise, went to trotting around the corral, head and tail up, and as tho no rider was on him, like he was plum free.

But after a spell of that the chestnut was made to act as tho there sure enough *was* a rider on him. In his own convincing way, Pete "sat down" on one rein and come near throwing the horse as he brought his head to "lay on his lap," then on the other side to do the same. The chestnut stopped in his tracks at that, like to sort of consider. Pete let him consider a spell, then with a light flip of his flat quirt started him again, at a crowhopping gait, and when that was over with and the horse lined out to trotting and walking around the corral, he stopped him again.

That was repeated a few times, and then Pete went to getting off and on him again and again, now without as much trouble as with an ordinary bronc. But too much of that don't do any good at first saddling, and if a bronc has only been caught, stopped, saddled, and rode, and hasn't got by with anything like bucking the saddle or rider off, or jerking away, and he's been made to do as the rider wanted, why that's all that's necessary for that first saddling.

The chestnut hadn't got by with anything, and Pete being satisfied of that got off of him once more and pulled the saddle off. The chestnut stood quiet. Then Pete pulled the hackamore off and opened the corral gate to the bronc pasture. The horse was now free to go, but he didn't make no snorting run for the open like most broncs do, he just walked along hardly looking at either side of him and when out of the corral a ways he stopped and looked back towards Pete who was watching him, the look in that chestnut's eyes was the same as when first roped, it went to both sides and beyond that cowboy, also like thru him.

"That horse is going to be either mighty good or mighty bad," says Pete as he closed the corral gate and made ready for the next bronc.

CHAPTER TWO

THE chestnut was corralled with the other broncs again the next day, and on account of Pete wondering more about him than he did the other broncs he caught him first, and if Pete wondered about the chestnut acting so different from other broncs he wondered some more as he dabbed his rope on him that second morning. He roped him by the neck this time and figuring that the horse would run on the rope, he took a turn around the snubbing post in the center of the round corral and would stop him quick so as to break him to never run on a rope or try to jerk away, but to Pete's surprise the chestnut hardly tightened the slack on the rope, and stopping turned to face him, with the same look as of the day before.

It came to Pete's mind again that somebody had already started to break the horse, but thinking of the happenings of the day before he figured that that couldn't be. For one thing the horse wouldn't of throwed himself over backwards as he had when front-footed, not unless he was a plum spoiled outlaw, and another thing, if he'd been handled before, outlaw or not, he wouldn't of fought the foot rope and hobbles the way he had if he'd once been made acquainted with 'em, and a horse of his breed would of had to been handled that way at first saddling. Pete knowed he sure hadn't been gentle broke, and the horse didn't act outlaw, just mighty odd and mysterious, and some scary for the rider on him in wondering what the samhill to expect from such a horse.

Not to be fooled by his quiet acting, Pete eased towards him and also in an easy way slipped the hackamore on his head, then flipped the end of the soft tie rope around his front feet and hobbled him. The horse quivered and snorted low but stood as tho glued to his tracks.

Still wondering, Pete reached for his saddle. He didn't think it necessary to tie up a hind foot to saddle him this time, not the way the horse acted so far. And it didn't seem necessary, for the horse only squatted a little as the saddle was eased on him and only kinked up some while his ears worked back and forth as the cinch was reached for and drawed up.

Pete whistled in wonder as that all was done so quiet like and rolled a smoke while the saddle "warmed" the chestnut's back, in July. With the hobbles still on his feet he turned him around once, like to just let him realize they was there and to sort of take away any hanker of bucking from the start. Then he took 'em off and without any more howdedo slipped in the saddle.

The chestnut's ears hardly moved as he did, and when there come a pull on the hackamore rein and the horse was started out of his tracks, he didn't make no wild leap as he did the day before. Instead he turned kind of easy and careful and made sure there was no ropes nor hobbles to trip him, then he ambled on around the corral, his ears not pointing back at the rider on him, nor pointing anywhere in particular, they was at peaceful and neutral angles.

Pete got off of him and opened the round corral gate into the big square corral, figuring that with more room that way the bronc would loosen up with whatever he might want to do, but as Pete got back on him that cowboy was near disappointed, for the chestnut acted as tho he was willing to do only what was wanted of him and there seemed to be less harm in him than there would be with a sugar-eating barn-yard pet. He didn't at all act like the range-bred horse of the kind that roams wild and sees a rider only once or twice a year.

There wasn't even the quiver of a muscle now as Pete got off of and back on him a few times, and his neck bent to the pull of the rein without a hint of his wanting to go against or fight it as an average bronc would.

Pete turned him this way and that way, walked him, trotted him and loped him in the big corral, stopped him short, started him and done more with him than with any horse he'd ever rode on second saddling. There wasn't any more he could do with the horse, for, according to contract he was only supposed to take the rough and fight out of the broncs. There sure didn't seem to be no more "rough" in the chestnut, and now it looked like he was ready for work and the finishing of his breaking with the handling of the herds. The easiest bronc that Pete had ever started.

He rode him in the big corral for a spell, and then he opened the corral gate. He would ride him outside in

The kind that roams wild and sees a rider only once or twice a year

the open, for there's when a bronc is most apt to turn loose and bring out everything that's in him, good or bad, stampeding or bucking. The open calls for freedom that way, specially at the first few saddlings.

But there again the chestnut was as docile as he'd been in the corral on that second saddling. It seemed like, as broncs sure enough do, that he'd thought things over thru the night from the first saddling, and that he'd decided to turn all to the good, making good use of his first lesson instead of scheming against it.

Pete rode him out for a mile or so and at all the different gaits from a standstill to a dead run, and when he rode him back in the corral, figuring that the horse had had more than an average setting for second saddling, and he unsaddled him, that cowboy shook his head in wonder. He'd never seen such a horse. But back of Pete's mind, and as he turned the chestnut out in the bronc pasture again, there was something which, from past experiences, kept a stirring. That horse was *too* good, and besides *he hadn't looked at him yet.*

The chestnut still didn't look at him when he was run in the next day for another saddling. But whether he looked at him or not that third saddling didn't seem at all necessary. As Pete caught him by the neck again, the horse turned to face him the second the loop drawed up on him. The hackamore was slipped on his head, and Pete didn't even bother to put the hobbles on him as he saddled him, and when he moved him out of his tracks and eased in the saddle it was like climbing on a good old cow-horse, only gentler than some.

It was monotonous and seemed useless to ride him around, getting off and on him and putting him thru the work the average bronc gets, for this horse acted as now ready to put in any man's string and to work with the herds, not as an ordinary bronc with just the rough took off of him but as a gentle horse, fitten for the poorest of riders or oldest and most busted up cowboy.

As he rode him around the corral and then outside, Pete near felt like "hooking" him, just to see if there was a buck left in him. He didn't like to see a bronc turn angel too quick, for he figured that the devil was in every bronc somewhere and the sooner it came out the better. He didn't like the devil to lay asleeping in 'em and show itself at the worst time and when a man is in a bad fix.

He rode the chestnut back in the corral, and rolled a smoke before unsaddling him. There was no use of riding that pony any more, he thought, for he acted as tho he could be trusted with anybody, anywhere, and any time. He would let him go for a few days now and take on another bronc in the place of him. There was no use of wasting any time on a gentle horse.

* * *

Four days went by when the chestnut run in the pasture and no saddle was put on his back. Then, thinking that something not too good might of hatched in that pony's mind in that time, Pete dabbed his rope on him one morning as he was run in.

There didn't seem to be no change in him much from

Pete got a vision of a murderous looking head mighty close to his face

the last time he was rode, only maybe a little snorty, but that was natural after so many days gone by without any saddling. A bronc can accumulate a lot of meanness in that time, no matter how gentle he might of been when last rode, where with a thoroly broke horse that length of time or longer would not make any difference. But even with his snorting and quivering a little when Pete came near to slip the hackamore on him, the chestnut didn't make no bad moves, and Pete eased the saddle on him as he did the last time, without hobbling him.

There was no bad move nor hump in his back as Pete pulled on the mecate and made him step out of his tracks, and he was near as quiet as before when the cowboy slipped into the saddle, let him stand a spell and then turned him into a start. All went about the same as the last time the horse was rode, only, Pete thought he felt the back muscles of that pony sort of stiffen and kink up every time he'd go to getting off and on him again, but he blamed that on his imagination, for the horse sure acted about as gentle as before. It seemed only a waste of time to be riding him any more, only maybe every few days or so.

But, wanting to satisfy himself about that kink in the back muscles, Pete figured he'd get off and get on him once more before unsaddling and turning him loose. He hobbled him so as to stand for a spell while he went into another corral, singled out another bronc and run him into the round corral.

When that was done the chestnut was still standing where he'd been left, not at all acting as tho he was concerned about anything, not until Pete came near and took the hobbles off of him and moved him a bit, then there was only a twitch of eye lid and an ear slanting to no perticular point.

Pete hardly thought of him as a bronc of only four saddlings as he stuck his boot toe in the stirrup and went to raise himself in the saddle. He thought again that he felt the muscles stiffen as he went to get into the saddle, and he was going to get back to the ground and get on again to make sure of that. Most of his weight was now in the left stirrup, and then, before his right leg touched the ground again all hell and damnation broke loose all at once and like coming out of the bowels of the earth itself. It was the chestnut. The devil in him had showed up sudden and the angel had evaporated just as sudden. A hind hoof caught Pete on the right knee and spinned him off his holt on the saddle horn and stirrup, but he'd went up with the horse, and as he was spun in the air, Pete got a vision of a murderous looking head mighty close to his face, and *the eyes was looking at him now.* Somehow or other he warded it off with his elbow and it missed him, but the point of the horse's shoulder caught him in the chest, a knee knocked the wind out of him, and as he hit the ground and his left leg flew up, a hind hoof caught it at the ankle and kicked it to snap limp.

The chestnut, now wild, blind mad and full of fight, bucked on over the unconscious Pete. It was wicked bucking and mighty well worth seeing as he circled around the corral and close to Pete a couple of times, and it was well that that cowboy wasn't up and a-standing right then, or he'd been made to hunt a hole and might of not got there in time. As it was the mad chestnut didn't pay no attention or maybe see him laying there. He bucked around the corral a few times and then hit straight for a heavy gate, crashed into and went thru it as tho it was made of toothpicks and then he was into another corral amongst many horses where he gradually cooled down and his ears finally pointed to neutral again. His eyes also got back that docile look.

Pete had trusted one bronc too far, but this chestnut was far from being an ordinary bronc.

CHAPTER THREE

PETE crawled to the bunk house on two hands and one knee. A ranch hand took him to the hospital in a light truck that afternoon and there he layed for two weeks. When he come out he was far from healed of his hurts, his left ankle had been well busted up and now was in a cast and his dislocated right knee was bandaged tight, but he wanted to get back to the ranch to recuperate. There would be chances of his getting to town again for treatment when he'd need to. Town was no fun for a cripple, and besides he wanted to be on hand to watch the show when some other rider would come along and take on his broncs where he left off. He was aching to see how the chestnut would act now after that sudden and unlooked for mad spree of his, and he wished he was able to find out for himself but it would be a few months before he would be in good enough shape to tackle that chestnut or any other bronc again and by that time there'd be no more broncs started, for the fall round-up and shipping would be about done and there wouldn't be enough work to keep the broncs going and make it worth starting any more that year. It would be hardened snow-bucking winter horses that would be needed from then on till spring.

So, as Pete took it easy, ruminated and read old magazines and saddlery catalogs in the bunk house or in the

It would be hardened snow-bucking winter horses that would be needed from then on till spring

shade of the big cottonwood in front of it, he wished every day that some new bronc peeler would pop up. He wanted to see a good one come so as the chestnut would have a chance to do his worst, for Pete seen now that with a second grade bronc peeler that chestnut wouldn't have a chance to really show his caliber, because a second grader would be put out of the way too quick.

Now, with himself, it would be another story if he was to handle that horse again. He wouldn't get careless and treat him as tho he was a gentle horse like he had when he got busted up. Yep, it sure would be another story, but he had to admit to himself that he'd be a little spooky handling that horse now because he was a vicious mystery to him. He just couldn't figure him out, and after another try he might come out in worse shape than he now already was.

Pete grinned as from under the big cottonwood he looked towards the corral. "Well, I started him anyhow, and a mighty good start too."

And being he'd started him and it was his place to name him, he now had one mighty good happening to go by, and a name came to him as to that horse's brand of character, a name that would fit, and identify him as well as the brand that was on his slick hide. The name was Scorpion.

With most all poisoned things like copperheads, sidewinders, trantlers, centipedes, hornets, and such a feller has a natural idea of where the poison fangs or stingers might be but with a scorpion it's where you'd least expect it, like with the chestnut's actions. The scorpion grabs with his front claws, but you don't get no poison from there, the poison stinger comes over his body at the tip of his curled up tail, and there you are.

From where you'd least expect it, and that's what the chestnut reminded Pete of doing things when least expected. So, Scorpion was the chestnut's starting name, and it stayed with him.

Long lonesome days went by for Pete, he was used to plenty of action. For company there was a couple of ranch hands who'd be gone all day and a China cook that "No savvy." A rider came in from round-up one evening, figuring on starting back the next morning with the broncs that Pete had been supposed to get the rough off, but as that hadn't been done according to contract, Pete said there was none and one look at him made it plain to see the reason why.

"I've got one started," says Pete. "Turned out as gentle as a frozen snake but he thawed out on me, and," waving a hand over his stove-up foot and leg, "this is what happened. I don't think the rough will ever be peeled off of him now. He'll be fit only for the rough string."

And the next morning as the rider went to leave, Pete says, "Tell that cow boss, Joe, to send a peeler over to finish taking the rough off of this string I've started, or else take 'em over to the 'wagon' (round-up outfit). They'll need quite a few more saddlings, some of 'em."

But before another rider came from the wagon there come another one, a stranger to that country but an old friend of Pete's. The two had rode many ranges together in other territories that was weeks' rides away.

The stranger had rode in about sun up, and Pete naturally wondering about this stranger's night riding had been the only one to see him and be at the door to holler at him. He'd recognized him by then, even if it had been a couple of years since he'd seen him. And the stranger, recognizing Pete soon as he turned to his holler liked to fell off his horse with surprise and pleasure. He did fall off but lit a-running and towards Pete.

But there was little talk, only mighty pleased grins, as the two shook hands, and Pete understanding his friend's secret-like look told him to come in the bunk house, it was the cowboys' bunk house and no ranch hands ever came in there much.

"But first," says Pete, "you'd better put your horse away while the hands are choring around at the stables." He pointed at the brushy creek bottom where tall grass stood. "You'll find some little clearings down there where you can either picket or hobble him and where nobody will be apt to see him."

While the stranger was gone, Pete, using a chair for a crutch went outside and hollered for the Chink, and when that Chink showed his "no savvy" face he hollered that he was much velly hungry this morning and for him to bring double feed, everything, lots of it and mucha quick.

As ornery as that Chink was he always paid good attention to Pete's orders. It was breakfast time anyway, and in a short while he brought over a whole pile of breakfast and a big pot of coffee, enough for two husky ranch hands, which amounts to about the same as enough for four wiry cowboys.

Pete seen the ranch hands leave the stable just as his friend came in the bunk house, and at the sight of the hot victuals spread on the old brand marked bunk house table the stranger snorted with pleasure.

"Dammit, old horse thief," he says, looking at the food, "this sure is fine. Ain't 'et for a day and a night and been riding like a wolf. Covered over a hundred miles since yesterday morning." He pointed at the grub. "How come a crippled cowboy to get this kind of care, chuck brought to him and all such? Never heard of or seen such a thing."

Pete seen the ranch hands come to the cook house which was off a ways, and after they'd walked in he told his friend to close the bunk house door. Then the two squared up to the table.

"Now we can talk, Tim," says Pete, "while we're storing up on this grub.—How come you to be riding nights when days are still so long, did somebody rub your fur the wrong way and make you take a pot shot at him?"

"Something like that," grins Tim, as he stabbed a slice of bacon, "only thing is I think I started it—The way it come about, I was riding on a passenger train on my way back from shipping cattle——"

"Yours?"

"Well—" Tim grinned again.

"Well, anyhow," he went on, "I was riding on a

passenger train, and coming acrost a long stretch of prairie one night the train stopped for no reason that I could see. I was out at the end of the coach, smoking and the train had stopped just a little while when I heard something like a muffled explosion and the train sort of shook a bit. I had a hunch of what was up, so I opens the door, and as I see the light from the open door of the express car I suspicioned it was a hold up, and sure enough. In a few seconds two men jump out of the express car, each carrying a big bag and pointing with the queerest looking guns you ever did see, there was a big black round something by the trigger guard. Another man jumps out from back of the engine and then, I don't know why, but I jumps out too and gets out a ways from the train to where I can see well. About then the train starts to pull out in a hurry, and there I am.

"But before the train had got well started I got a good look at the lit up inside of the express car and I seen two men standing inside with their arms away up.

"I might of tried to've caught the train and went on about my business but these two hold up fellers outside raised their queer looking guns and went to smoking up the two railroad men and shot 'em down right there, and them with their hands up and harmless.

"Well, that got me to boiling and mighty interested, and I forgot about the train going on. It's a wonder I didn't start smoking up on them two hombres soon as I seen what they was up to, but I couldn't understand that kind of a game, such as shooting men who's got their hands up. The harm was done when I come to realize, and being sort of foolish that way I thought I'd sort of even scores.

"It was a pretty dark night, but getting down to the ground and winding towards the bad hombres thru the low brush I got to where I could see them against the sky. The gazabo that'd been at the engine had joined 'em by then, and the three got to talking. The bags and their guns was beside 'em on the ground."

Pete had stopped eating, for his interest had got the best of his appetite. He just drank coffee and smoked and listened. Tim went on pretty well with his eating while he talked, only once in a while stopping to point a fork or a knife and make a few motions. He was storing up quite a feed.

"I got to thinking while they talked, what was their scheme for making their get away, they didn't seem to be in a hurry or fretting any, and now, what the samhill should I do with 'em, not at all thinking of what they might do with me, you know I'm sort of dumb that way. Anyhow I got to thinking I sure couldn't shoot 'em down as they did them two express men, and I didn't want to parade 'em in to jail, I'd of felt like a stool pigeon or something as small. I would let the officers of the law get 'em, that's their business and I figured they would get 'em quick enough.

"I'd cooled down some by then, but I had to do something to sort of even up scores for what I thought was a dirty trick. Then it came to me. I could take their guns away from 'em so they couldn't at least shoot anybody for a while, and the police might get 'em

I could see their paws well up against the sky

before they got more guns and ammunition, then if all went well I'd take the loot they'd got. That would be sort of discouraging to 'em, and the scare I would give 'em would cap that off well and jibe with the old saying that crime never pays. That would be evening scores for the men they shot down, I thought, giving 'em a good lesson to boot and making them easier and harmless to catch. No money and no guns."

Tim pointed his fork at a seven-inch barrel, 45 six shooter a-hanging close at his side. "I eased this little old iron out of my pants belt, filled the one empty chamber and then crawled closer. I didn't know if they'd do as I told 'em to or not, so when I told 'em to 'put 'em up' from one place I was in another place quicker than you could say 'scat,' and when they seemed to hesitate I let go of a slug that sprinkled gravel all over 'em. I could hear it scatter on the canvas express bags.

"They didn't hesitate no more from then and I could see their paws well up against the sky. Then I told 'em to move away from where they was. I'd changed places again and my voice too, so I guess they figured there must of been at least two men bearing down on 'em.

"I wondered afterwards how come they didn't just drop to earth when I first spoke to 'em and go to shooting, and I figured they just wasn't used to shooting it out in the open.

"But anyhow, I was in another place and using another voice when I told 'em to take off their coats careful and drop 'em to the ground. I was thinking of them patent automatics I heard them kind of fellers packed.

"I was three men at about that time, and I guess they figured they was pretty well covered because they was careful in taking off their coats, careful not to feel for the pockets.

"I was running short on changes of voices about then but I managed another one and told 'em to move away from there too. From all appearances they was down to their shirtsleeves, their arms up again and I couldn't see no signs of guns as I got low to the ground and looked over their outlines against the sky.

"I didn't have much to fear then, I didn't think. But now I got to thinking again, what was I going to do with 'em, make 'em hit out afoot? About then I seen the lights of a car a-coming like a bat out of hell and I could make out a highway not far from the railroad track. It comes to me then that that was a car to come and pick 'em up and as to their plans for their getaway. That relieved me some, and then I says to 'em in my natural voice. It was all right for me to use my own voice now because I figured I could easy enough be one of the four men I'd changed my voices and places to. So I says to 'em, 'You fellers get in that car when it stops and keep on a-going.'

"The car had come to a stop by then. The door was opened for 'em and them two-bit gunmen sure wasn't slow clambering in, all excepting one who stops to ask at the door, 'Is that you and your gang, Pete?'

"That name of yours near got me in bad because I come near laughing and answering right from where I stood, and that sure would of gave 'em a chance to go to shooting the direction of my voice if there was a gun in the car, which there was. So instead of answering by words I let my old cannon talk, you know how it can talk and roar and convince. I shot twice just like one shot, scattered gravel all over that freak and the car, and the sound of my second shot hadn't died out when I was some good distance from where I'd shot.

"There I shot once more and as quick as tho there'd been another man shooting with me, and as luck protects the young and the dumb I'd bellied up along side of a nice sized boulder about two feet high and plenty long, right between me and the car. But I didn't need the protection of that good old rock because there wasn't one shot come from the direction of the cake eating desparadoes. From there I spoke and ordered them to throw out all guns and ammunition or I'd cut the car in two and them with it. They was mighty obedient and done that quick. I don't think they even kept one pea shooter, not by the size of the pile of guns they left by the road.

Then I told 'em to get going, but they seemed to've got mighty excited and the driver couldn't get the car in gear, not until I let go another good slug at the top of it. I heard glass a shattering and then the car lunged in a buck jump and it sure went from there. But not before I let fly another shot at the gas tank.

"I watched the car go till I couldn't see the light of it no more, to make sure they didn't slow down and come back afoot or in the car with the lights off. But they sure burned the road, didn't slow down no time, and on that flat prairie I know they was quite a few miles away by the time I couldn't see the lights of the car no more.

"And I wasn't still while I watched that car either, nor did I waste any time as to what I should do now. I come to where they'd shed off their coats and, sure enough there was iron weights in all three of 'em, good sized automatics, and I left all that rigging lay as it was. Then I got to the express bags and the queer looking rifles. I didn't bother examining them rifles for fear I'd shoot myself with the deformed contraptions, so I let them lay where they was. But with the bags it was different. I sure couldn't leave 'em lay there, somebody might come along and appropriate 'em, so I took 'em.

"Them two bags was pretty heavy, but thinking them fellers might come back or somebody else might come, I left that spot in a hurry and packed the bags for near a mile acrost the prairie and straight away from the railroad and highway.

"There I stopped and investigated the bags. Both of 'em was locked, but there'd been a hole cut at the top, then in one of the bags I felt a square leather case and I got it out. It had been locked too but the lock had been pried loose, and raising the cover I felt stacks of what I thought was money. So I lit a match inside my hat to see, and sure enough, they was bills all tied up and in packages of ten to each, all ranging from twenty on up to hundred dollar bills. That leather box was steel lined and it was plum full of such bills. I figure there must be around thirty thousand dollars in it."

"What did you do with the box?" asks Pete, as tho he wasn't caring much.

I sure couldn't leave 'em lay there, somebody might come along and appropriate 'em

Tim grinned at him as hc drank some coffee. "Well, there's where I made my mistake and why I'm riding nights," he says. "I took it along. I buried it night before last about a hundred miles from here.

"If I'd been smart I'd of maybe sat close by where the hold up had took place and waited till the officers come.

I should of maybe held them bad eggs there too because I found out afterwards that them officers wasn't slow getting there. If I'd done that I could of most likely collected a good reward, got a lot of pats on the back and wouldn't be in the predicament I'm in now.

"But I don't care for any reward or blood money so I thought I'd just take that leather box to sort of repay myself for the chances I'd took in scattering them hold up fellers and so it would be well taken care of. I at least took their guns away from 'em. They couldn't shoot anybody now and they didn't have any money to get very far with, I don't think, besides there might of been something in the coats I made 'em leave that would identify 'em. So I felt I was justified all around and didn't do anybody any harm, and as for the money, they'd of got it if I hadn't been there, and used it to buy more ammunition, make up bigger gangs and kill more people, where with me it'll only go to distribution in making everybody happy, in women and song and good horses. Then you can't tell, I might buy me some good little outfit and settle down somewhere."

"That would sure surprise you and me both," grins Pete. "But you'd better not be on the dodge when you do. How far are they behind you now, you think?"

"Who?" asks Tim.

"Why, them that's on your trail."

"There's nobody on my trail yet that I know of."

"But you said something about being in a predicament."

"Oh, yeh. Well I meant—I am in a predicament,

because I took that money and now I don't know how close any officer might be to me, nor how far or if there's any on my trail as yet. If there ain't I think there'll soon be, all on account of my dumbness too, because as soon as I got the money box I hit back for the highway with it and finally got a car to stop and pick me up. There was one lone young feller driving the car and he spotted that queer looking leather case first thing.

"He said something about it being sort of odd looking and asked me what I used it for, just like some kid, you know. Well I thought a bit and then I told him I was gathering some special specimens of rocks for some university and that I used the case to ship them in. I was afraid he'd want to see 'em but he didn't and I was glad when after about an hour's ride he dropped me off at the depot in a good sized town.

"But that young feller acted sort of suspicious and if he got to hearing about the hold up after he left me at the depot and got to thinking it had been pulled off at about the place where he'd picked me up, then my queer looking case and all, he'd be mighty apt to tell about me. He had a good chance to get my description too.

"Besides that there's the young hold up fellers which are sure to be caught and as sure to tell on me or the four men that held them up, and even tho they didn't get my description there's my boot heels tracks all over that gravelly ground down there, and anybody can see they was made by only one man.

"So sooner or later there'll be somebody on my trail and I don't know how soon.

"When the young feller left me off at the depot I went to the express window. It was open and a man was there listening to his telegraph apparatus. He seemed excited and after he got thru listening he went on to do some ticking of his own. I waited at the window, after he got thru he turned, and being I was the only one around he says to me, 'My God, mister, number eight has been held up and two special guards have been killed.' He squinted at me for a bit and I was glad I'd dropped the case to the floor at my feet where he couldn't see it. Then he went on, not squinting at me no more. 'The hold up was committed by three young men of around twenty, all well dressed and supposed to be part of such and such a gang.' I forget the name.

"Anyhow I didn't seem to fit as to such description. I'd went to that window to get some paper to wrap up the suspicious looking leather box but I thought better of doing that there right then. So I waited till he turned to the clicking of his telegraph again and then I eased out with my money box. I was kind of spooky by then and I know that some of the depot men must of seen that box but it couldn't be helped, I'd had no chance to wrap or disguise it in any way.

"Soon as I got out of the depot I hit acrost the street to about the only open place I could see. It was about three in the morning by then. The place was a Chink restaurant, and producing two bits I finally got the paper and string to wrap and tie the doggone box.

"I felt a little better then but some skittish again when I got to the depot and I was sure glad the box was covered up and didn't weigh much, because by then the few people that was there, they was mostly all depot and train men, had all heard about the hold up and was all a-jabbering like a bunch of excited monkeys. The best thing I thought for me to do then was to join the party and act interested. I was interested, specially to hear how the goings on of the hold up was so already twisted and made worse. I thought I might hear something of the hold up or the hold up men, by the 'four men,' you know, but I guess it was too soon for that yet and that wouldn't come out till the four well dressed ginks got caught.

"I was glad to find out later that there was a train heading my direction in a couple of hours, and even tho the waiting was kind of long and uncomfortable it was sure better than fitting the description of the three I'd made scatter, specially with the package of mine.

"As it was, with my boots on, a hand-me-down suit and my little Dakota hat over my mop of uncut hair and then my sunburnt physog, I figured I wouldn't of at all be given even a first glance as a suspect of the hold up. But the 'toot' of the old train sounded mighty good to me as it finally come a-rambling on. I'd got me another ticket because the part of the one I had would of needed too much explaining and bring on too much attention, specially at the time and place where I'd quit using it. I'd also got stylish and wanted to hide so I got me a berth too, and soon as I got into that dark Pullman, got my ticket punched and found my berth I wasn't so spooky no more. Maybe I was too tired. Anyhow I just pulled my boots off, got the money box close to my short ribs and by my smoke wagon and went right into slumberland.

"Well, to make a long story as short as I can, I filled up good on the train and before I got to the town where I was headed I had some sandwiches made up, and when I got off at that town that afternoon I didn't linger none there but hit straight for the livery stable where I'd left my horse and outfit before shipping the cattle.

"Nobody had seemed to heard of the hold up at that town as yet, not at the stable anyway because the few that was around was still talking about nothing in particular when I got there. It was a good time for me to hit out, before everybody heard and got to watching everybody else, and that same afternoon I hit for the hills, good old rough hills where nothing but cayotes and jack rabbits ever run. After locating a good place in some thick brush and where it would never wash, I waited till near dark and started digging a good hole with a hard stick, scraping the dirt out with my hands, then I took about a thousand dollars out of the box, for travelling expenses, you know, and I slipped the box, paper and all, in its resting place, covered it with some dirt, placed a big rock on top and then scattered the rest of the dirt around with some branches and to mix natural with all around. I sure spotted me a good landmark too, a sharp peak that sticks up at a little distance and which I can see for fifty miles from any direction, and I could find the spot where the 'treasure' is if I was blindfolded.

"Well, that's about all, except that when I left the spot it was mighty dark and I zigzagged a plenty in the rough, rocky country before I headed for the flats, then I hit for a well-travelled road where my tracks would be well covered on the next day.

"As the sun got well up that day, that was yesterday, I left the road before there was any travel on it and hit for a brushy creek bottom where I watered my horse and let him graze, and there I et the sandwiches I'd got on the train. I was about sixty miles from the town then, and around forty from where I'd cached the money box. Good start, I thought, nobody in sight from where I'd come and everything clear to where I was headed. I done some careful and fast riding from the time I left that creek bottom yesterday morning and used all my tricks to cover up my trail. I think I done that well and made it hard to follow. I seen a few riders and automobiles during the day but none seen me."

He refilled his cup with coffee, turned his chair from the table, and rolling a smoke, he went on. "And now here I am, my horse is getting his, and the best of all is riding into you like this. I never thought you'd be in this country and it's sure a good surprise for me to see you and talk to you again. I sort of missed your ornery company."

"Yeh," says Pete, half peeved like, "and here you come looking over your shoulder and ready to jump any minute. You'll have to ride out of the country and dodge now, just when I need you here and there's a good job finishing taking the rough off the broncs I've started. You always have to put up the flank cinch first and undo it last as usual."

Tim grinned. "You're wrong there, Pete, old boy. I've improved some since you seen me last, amongst which I've sort of quit riding the rough ones, too rough on a feller, plenty elevating in some ways but sort of standing still in other ways. Yep, I've graduated from such as riding broncs. But," he went on after a while, "I might help you out with one if he's tough enough and I can ride him out of the country."

CHAPTER FOUR

TIM hid out in the creek bottom near to where his horse was eating and resting, sprawled out on the grass by his saddle, and not at all minding the mosquitoes that swarmed in the damp shady place, went to sleep, the sleep of a he wolf in his den while his mate watched the entrance.

Pete was in the shade of the cottonwood by the bunk house and where he could pretty well see the road and trails leading into the ranch, his legs was stretched out on a bench and an old magazine layed open on his lap, a peaceful picture of comfort while recuperating. But his eyes hardly seen the magazine and, near like the chestnut, Scorpion's, the corners of 'em was on both sides of it to the roads and trails that was in sight. A special holler from Pete would get Tim up on his feet and watchful, no matter how sound he'd be sleeping at the time.

Tim was resting while Pete was watching and thinking, thinking of ways to help his friend out for a clean getaway. It didn't matter much to him what Tim had done, for that cowboy was always into something anyway, and if he done any foolishness he done enough good in other and different ways to more than make that up. Now, Pete figured that if Tim was witness or connected with the hold up in any way and was suspicioned of taking the money box and they had his description where the hold up was pulled off, he could easy enough be traced to the town where he got off the train and to the stable where he got his horse. From there his trail would be hard to follow, but with the many men that would be on it, quite a bit of country for a long ways could be covered in a short time, until some clue was found as to the direction Tim had taken, then they'd get together and work mighty fast in that direction.

But somehow, Pete didn't have much fear of anybody being on Tim's trail for a few days, or maybe nobody would be on his trail, and not until the hold up men was caught. But they might be caught by now. He would see that evening if he could get one of the ranch hands to drive the light ranch truck to the post office. It was only twenty miles away, at a ranch and general store on the county road, and a late newspaper could be got there. He could send the ranch hand with the excuse he expected some medecine from town, and to get a couple of newspapers, just to see what was going on in the world.

It was early afternoon when Tim came out of the creek bottom and up to where Pete had been sitting. Another big meal had been brought by the Chink, and even tho it had cooled some, Pete had covered everything so the meal was a feast as compared to what a man gets while on the dodge, or in jail.

Pete hadn't touched the meal, only some of the coffee, saying that a man sure loses his appetite sitting around and doing nothing, but Tim made him eat some,

Tim hid out in the creek bottom near to where his horse was eating and resting

the soup and other things. "I need something solid and which'll stick to my ribs," he says.

As they et they went on from where the conversation had left off that morning, about things in general from when and where they'd been and what they'd done since they'd last seen one another, how Pete come to get so busted up, and then that talk came to the present and as to the best thing to do and where to go from here.

"The first thing I ought to have," says Tim, while on that subject, "is a change of horses. I've crowded this horse of mine pretty hard from the start. He's tired and it wouldn't take him long to get leg weary. Then again this horse of mine is too well known and with the brand on him he would identify me too well, specially from the stable where I last rode him out of. Yep, I need a change of horses, color, brand and all, then I'd sort of be leaving a cold trail, which would be coming to an end soon as I change horses, and I'd be starting out on a fresh trail that'd be mighty hard to follow— so if you've got a good tough horse that you'd sell, loan, or trade me why point him out to me. I'd leave my gray here with you and he's yours. You won't have to worry about anybody claiming that horse because I bought and paid for him. You know the horse, I started breaking him before you left the outfit down there, and you know he's sure turned out good or I wouldn't still be having him. The horse is not known up here in this country, he couldn't be identified as mine only by the stable man, and turned out in some out of the way pasture or range for a spell he'd never be paid any attention to. But if I was to be riding him thru the country and the stable man gave the description of that horse and me together, why it'd make it harder to cover my trail in case I was seen now and again."

"Yes, I savvy," says Pete, who'd listened well and thought right along on the subject, "but what's bad is that I haven't got a horse of the kind you need. I've got them two old pets of mine, you know them too. I've been using them only to go from one outfit to another to get work or to go to town once in a while. They haven't been rode since I got this job early last spring, and they're as fat as fools and strong, but they're a little too old for the wild ramblings you might want to do or have to do. There ain't a horse here on the ranch that'd do either, only the broncs I've started and a couple of old has-beens the ranch hands use to irrigate or ride fence with once in a while."

Well, that didn't set so good with Tim. But there was nothing could be done about it, and he knowed that Pete would sure let him have a horse if he had a good one to give. No bronc could stand a long ride every day and the only gentle horses was too old, so that was that.

Tim grinned at the serious look on Pete's face. "Never mind, old boy," he says to him, "I'll ride on with my gray. I'll get to trade him for another good horse easy enough—but there'd be a snag there, for whoever gets my gray horse would have the description of the horse I'd traded him for and I'd be in about the same fix as if I kept my gray. I would like to get a horse from somebody who wouldn't tell what kind of a horse I rode away on so my trail would sort of end with the gray. Besides I'd sure hate to leave this horse of mine with a stranger."

The while Tim was talking Pete was doing some more tall thinking. His eyes gazed the direction his horses ranged and he tallied up in his mind what other horses run out there with his, and come to figure that none would do. Then he gazed back to the ranch, down to the bronc pasture and just as a few of the broncs came into sight from a watering place. He easy recognized Scorpion among 'em, and at the sight of him his face lit up sudden. But it wasn't for long, and he finally shook his head. No, that horse wouldn't do.

But Tim caught him at the head shaking and he asked him what he'd decided against now. Pete grinned at that.

"Oh," he says, "I just happened to think of a horse that might do but he wouldn't."

"Why?" asks Tim, pleased that there might be one chance.

"He's crooked," says Pete. "Gentle as a stuffed owl one minute and vicious as a she lion with sixteen kittens the next." He pointed at his bandaged leg and foot in cast. "He's the one that done this."

But with all proof of the meanness of that horse, mean and tricky enough so as to get such a bronc peeler as Pete down, Tim wasn't at all put out or leary.

"How old is he?" he asks, "old enough to stand a good ride?"

"Yes, he's a good age, five going on six, and I think he'll stand a ride as well as any good broke horse because he won't wear himself out bucking or fighting the bit. He's mighty strong and tough and can't easy be hurt in no way. But, as I said before, he'll make you think you're riding the old home pet while you're really sitting on dynamite, and you never can tell when he might explode."

Tim slapped his leg and whooped, "That's the horse for me." He grins, happy, "Keep a feller awake."

But Pete was serious when he says, "No, Tim, he's no horse for a feller that's on the dodge and I can't let you have him. He'd stomp on you and cripple you when you need him the most, or maybe scatter your brains all over the side of some mountain when you're the most at ease and at peace and the least expecting."

"Well, that's cheerful to think about, and I'm glad you warned me, that'll keep me all the more awake, and if he can stand a good ride he's still the horse for me." He grinned some more. "You ain't got nothing to say and there's nothing you can do about it, not in the fix you're in, so I'm going to relieve you of all blame and responsibilities and just appropriate that horse wether you like it or not. I'll leave my gray with your horses in the place of him and you can fix it up with the company any way you see fit."

But Pete only shook his head, serious. "I'm sorry I mentioned him," he says, "and I'm sure advising you not to fool with him, specially at this time. I'd be worried stiff about you."

You and me used to swap broncs in the hills or any place and we had a lot of fun doing that

Tim also got serious. "Why, what's the matter with me?"

"Well, there was nothing the matter with me either until I bumped up against that horse."

"Oh, that was just on account you didn't get to know the horse and trusted him too much. But you know him now, and I'll have a better chance than you did because you warned me. I won't go to sleep on him, don't worry—but right now and here is where I need to change horses, where nobody will describe the horse I'll be changing to nor tell of the direction I take. —And another thing," Tim went on, "you and me used to swap broncs in the hills or any place and we had a lot of fun doing that. Now there's going to be another swap and there never was no better reason nor time for one. I understand the horse needs riding bad, I need the horse bad, and being you won't be able to ride him for a long time I can sure make good use of him in that time and keep him from spoiling."

Tim was for going to run the chestnut in right away and try him out, but Pete advised him against that too, saying that he'd better think it over till morning. That he'd been expecting a rider from the wagon every day and he'd be more apt to show up in the afternoon than any time, so might any other rider.

"You better keep hid all you can and rest up till tomorrow morning. Tonight you can go in the store-room and supply up on some grub to do you till you get a good distance away and where it might be safe to show yourself at some old sourdough's camp, where there's no telephone and you could dicker for another light supply of salt and rice and jerky."

"Wise advice and wisely said," grins Tim. "And now I'll have time to manicure my fingernails and put a wave in my hair."

"And fill up," Pete adds on.

When the ranch hands came in that evening it was more than agreeable with one of them to go to the post office after supper was thru, for, as the other ranch hand remarked, that feller was getting regular mail from a certain female and was always anxious to get it.

So, as the car was heard returning just a little after dark, it was also an anxious Tim who was outside while the papers was brought in to Pete. Then as the ranch hand drove the car on to put it away he made a dive into the bunk house, closed the door and went to Pete who was now hard at perusing the papers.

"They've got 'em," Pete says, first thing, "caught 'em the next day and just about the time you was getting off the train, five hundred miles from where they was caught and where the hold up was pulled off. It says here they run out of gas only about twenty miles from where they'd held up the train. There was a leak in their gas tank." Pete looked at Tim who was looking at the paper over his shoulder. "Maybe made by some of the gravel your shots splattered on the car," he says, "or did you aim at the gas tank?"

"Well, I aimed at one corner of it."

Pete grinned and went on reading the paper, which went on to say that the car had been towed to the out-

The paper went on to tell how it was expected that one of the four men would soon be apprehended

skirts of a town by a passing car; the passengers in the car had noticed the shattered glass in the bandits' car, looked like made by a bullet, also the hole at one corner of the gas tank. It looked kind of queer for the men to be in their shirt sleeves too, and, as the car that towed 'em in went on into town to a filling station and its passengers heard of the train hold up which had been pulled just a couple of hours before, the car and the men they'd towed in naturally came to their mind and they told the filling station man about that.

That was like setting a match to a bomb, and the men was caught by officers who came out on foot and followed the one who'd walked into town to get a can of gas, while the others was plugging the hole in the gas tank.

In jail, the men confessed of the hold up but denied having any part in the shooting of the express guards, that the "four men" who'd in turn held them up had done that shooting, with the guns they'd taken away from 'em.

Pete and Tim looked at one another mighty serious like.

"Yeow," says Tim, finally, "now I am a sure enough outlaw, and I will need a change of horses bad."

The paper went on to mention about the "DARING DOUBLE HOLD-UP" that a strong box containing $40,000 in currency had been taken by the four men who'd held up the bandits, but that there was one redeeming feature about them four men, for they hadn't touched the estimated $20,000 in the registered mail and packages, none had been opened and the bags had been placed to where they could easy be found, near the young gangsters' coats and guns.

"More money in that box than I thought," says Tim to that, "I thought of the registered mail and packages, too, but I also thought of the many people that money was being sent to, some in hospitals maybe, others stranded in strange places and maybe hungry, and then others that'd need the money mighty bad to put over some good honest deal. No, Pete, I couldn't touch that money."

"You wouldn't make a very good outlaw," says Pete, and both went on reading the same paper some more.

Another redeeming feature about the four men, the paper says, was that they'd disarmed the bandits who, desperate as they seemed, would of most likely resisted arrest and killed or injured some of the officers and others in trying to make their escape.

"Well, that's something," says Tim, sort of proud.

"Yeh, but look a here," says Pete.

The paper went on to tell how it was expected that one of the four men would soon be apprehended. He'd be a valuable witness against the bandits and he'd have a lot to explain for himself and his companions. There'd been tracks from high heeled riding boots around the bandits' guns and express bags, and as them tracks had been traced the officers had been puzzled because the tracks showed as being made by only *one man*, and *not four*.

The description of the one man had been furnished by a local resident of such and such a town who, driving along the highway, had stopped to pick him up and drove him to the depot of another town. The man he'd picked up looked to be a cowboy, of medium height and lean, and carrying a leather-covered boxlike case, which had been described to fit with the express money box.

That box had also been noticed by a few depot employees, and from them it had been learned that the man had bought a ticket and took a train headed west.

"You see," says Tim, "there's where I made my mistake, packing that money box around the way I did, and showing myself near the place of the hold up. If I'd of had any brains I'd of hit out afoot on the hard road where my tracks would of soon been covered by cars, buried the box along the way somewhere or took it with me and wrapped it up first chance I got. I would of dodged all cars and walked the rest of the way into town, and I could of made it by morning I think, and then I could of got me a pair of shoes and a cap, and I'd been ready to hop on the train, nobody noticing me.

"But the law has a way of finding them things out mighty quick, and maybe I'd been caught up with before I got disguised and to the depot, or I might of had to dodge in that strange country, afoot, which would put me in a heap worse fix than I'm in now.

"The whole thing is that I wasn't out to commit no crime nor get mixed up in any hold up and I didn't do much thinking. It just came sudden that I'd have a little fun scattering them bandits, and then, like after chasing a bunch of cayotes from a fresh kill I just took a wolf's share of what they'd downed and went on about my business without looking back."

Pete had to grin at that. "You got the wolf's share all right," he says. Then he went on, serious. "But it looks to me like you'll have to do a heap of tall riding and dodging for a long time and a long ways so as to get any good out of that box of money. It won't give you no rest. It'll be spent careless and you'll still be on the dodge, with your heart up your gizard every time you see somebody. Then supposing you want to settle down to one place some day, as you say you might."

"You're sure a cheerful cuss," says Tim, grinning a little. "But it's done now, old boy, can't undo 'er."

"Oh, I don't know," Pete comes back at him. "Have you ever thought of returning the box with all the money, and shed clear of the whole mess?"

"Yes, I thought of that a bit, until now when I see by this paper that the cayotes I made scatter are pinning the murdering of the two guards onto me. There'd be four of them against one of me swearing to that, and things can be so all twisted up sometimes that way that I might wind up a-sitting in one of them chairs where they have you set for a spell and cart you off afterwards, deader than door nailed.

"No, Pete, I think I'll hang on to my scalp and stick to good horses and open country as long as I can, and finish what I started. I'll maybe get used to being on the dodge, and as things quiet down and it's found out that it's them cayotes themselves who done the murdering, which I think will be found out, why there won't be apt to be many on my trail. Anyhow, right now would sure be a poor time for me to show up with the money and try to explain. I'd be locked up first thing, and with the people being so all up in the air and rearing to go I might not get a chance to explain much, or believed if I did."

"Yes, I guess maybe you're right there," agreed Pete.

"Besides I know of a country that if I can get to it I won't be worried much about anybody riding in on me. It's good wild horse country and nothing else much, and after things cool down I'll ride back and get the money I've buried up here, then I'll have decided as to what to do with it."

"That'll be all right, if it works that way," says Pete.

"I'll ride for it, cowboy, and so it will work that way," answers Tim. "I guess you know me when I ride for anything."

The two went back to perusing the papers, and as they read on they noticed that nothing was said about what town the man (Tim) had been headed for nor if officers had followed him there. That hadn't been necessary of course, but Tim would of liked to've known because he'd bought a ticket to a destination of quite a few hundred miles beyond where he got off, where his horse was. He'd liked to've known if they'd be looking for him where he'd bought the ticket to or where he really got off.

"I think they'll find that out pretty quick," says Pete, "but that might give you an extra day."

"Yes," says Tim, looking sort of grim-like, "and maybe I've used that day."

He stood up, rolled a smoke and walked around a bit, then he turned to Pete who was still reading.

"I'm riding tonight, Pete," he says, "and I'm riding Scorpion."

CHAPTER FIVE

A NEW moon was sinking as Tim, on his gray horse, brought the broncs from the pasture and corralled 'em. By that time, Pete had made good use of a chair and a stick and was down at the corrals, and before the new moon sunk over the mountain to the west he pointed out the Scorpion horse to Tim.

"If you're still in mind to ride him," says Pete, "that's him over there next to the corral. The one with the bowed neck."

In answer, Tim made a loop, and from his horse let it sail to settle over the roman nosed head and drawed it up on the bowed neck. There was a beller of surprise from the chestnut, he bogged his head and made a couple of buck jumps, then snorting at the new and strange way of being caught, from the back of another horse, he turned and stood tense, head high and all watchful.

Leaving his rope tied hard and fast to the saddle horn, Tim got off his gray and went along that rope towards the chestnut. In his right hand was the soft foot rope Pete had been using, and getting close to the chestnut he dropped it so it'd be within easy reach, then he raised his hand easy towards the "knowledge bump" between that horse's ears. That always was Tim's first aim when first coming up to a bronc, and as he'd say, "Once they let you touch that bump you've got 'em."

His hand was near the side of Scorpion's left eye aiming for the bump when Pete, who'd never before thought of ever warning Tim about any bronc, spoke up.

"Better watch out for that arm of yours," he says.

He'd no more than spoke when Scorpion's teeth bared on it. But Tim sort of expected that and lost only a small piece of his shirt sleeve and a little skin. He also expected the front hoof that flew up at about the same time and missed him by only a few inches, for that double action sort of comes together. Scorpion then backed against the rope and went to fighting it, rearing and pawing at it. The good gray horse held him easy, and gave just enough on the rope so the chestnut wouldn't choke himself.

Tim, with his left hand on the tight rope, and keeping himself just clear from the pawing hoofs, reached down for the soft rope, and turning to Pete who was sitting on his "crutch" chair in the shadows, he says,

"Thought you said this was a extraordinary bronc. He acts like any ordinary green one to me. I'd say at about the fourth saddling."

"Right," says Pete, "this will be the fifth. But wait till he starts playing possum on you and gets you to thinking he's as gentle as Mary's little lamb. Then's when he'll be apt to get you."

"Thanks for reminding me, old boy. I'll watch out for that, and I wish he would play some of that possum on me right now because he'll be needing this action he's wasting. You said he wouldn't fight much."

There was a beller of surprise from the chestnut, he bogged his head and made a couple of buck jumps

"Well, he didn't only a little the first time I caught him. At second and third saddling he was gentler than your gray, and at the fourth saddling too until I was about ready to unsaddle him and turn him out. Then's when he busted loose. I wished he'd acted the way he's acting now and right along until I got it out of him, then I wouldn't of got so careless."

"I won't get careless no matter how he acts," says Tim; "not after knowing what he has done to you."

Scorpion had quit his fighting and come to a standstill, all a-quiver and ready to blow up again as Tim came near him, flipped one end of the soft rope around his ankles and made a double half hitch around the both of 'em, then another hitch in the center and the horse was hobbled tight.

Tim wished the slice of moon would stay up a little longer but it was fast sinking and only a tip showed over a low ridge. But Pete, from where he was sitting, could well see the slant of Scorpion's ears, at a peaceful angle but a danger sign from *that* horse. He drawed Tim's attention to that fact, and Tim noticing, remarked:

"Yeh. That would sort of get an unsuspecting feller all right."

"But wait till you see his eyes in day time, they're still more peaceful and docile looking than the slant of them ears might lead you to think."

"Thanks again, Pete. I'll know this Scorpion better than you do if you keep on. And I've got something for them pretty eyes of his which I think will sort of leave him in the dark."

He went to his gray and took the hackamore off his head, leaving only the split ear bridle. On the hackamore was a three inch wide, latigo leather brow band. That brow band could be lowered to fit well over the horse's eyes and used as a blindfold if needed. Few cowboys ever use a blindfold because once it's used while breaking a bronc it will take a long time, and the bronc will have to be pretty well gentled, before he can be saddled and mounted without that blindfold over his eyes.

Tim kept the blindfold on his hackamore always, and even tho he seldom used it on broncs he'd found it pretty handy on older spoiled horses when getting on or getting off of 'em in scary places, where the horse had all the advantage and the rider none.

Being hobbled, Scorpion only slid back a little on his front feet as Tim came near him and begin slipping the hackamore on his head. The horse could of struck with both front feet even tho hobbled and as some broncs do, but ropes around the ankles takes a lot of fight out of any bronc, and Tim didn't have no trouble slipping the hackamore on Scorpion's head. Then he pulled the blind down over his eyes and at that the horse only stood and trembled, lost as to what to do and where to aim.

"I don't give a doggone what he does after I get in the middle of him," says Tim to Pete; "it's this arguing on the ground with a bronc's hoofs that I don't like."

He went to his gray horse again, untied the rope

from the saddle horn, unsaddled him and packed his saddle to the snubbing post. There in a flour sack was a light bundle of grub which he'd gathered from the store room and had all ready to tie onto the saddle. He done that, making sure it wouldn't loosen from any kind of a jolt, then he packed the saddle near the chestnut, slipped the blanket on his back, then the saddle, and cinched it. Scorpion quivered and flinched at every touch but never moved.

"Well, I guess it's all ready for the fireworks," he says as he took the rope off the chestnut's front feet and moved him out of his tracks. Then, with the movement of a cougar and without putting hardly any weight in the stirrup he eased in the saddle, and reaching ahead he pulled up the blind.

He was sitting well in the saddle, and while Scorpion blinked to get his bearings he pulled his head to one side to sort of take the bucking notion out of him. But that only seemed to bring it on, and so sudden and wicked that Tim come near losing his rigging (saddle).

A first hard jolt from a standstill is more apt to loosen a rider than if the hard jolts came on after a few easier ones from the start. As the first hard jolt loosened Tim he was surprised and jolted a plenty more, for, now sort of set for more to come the horse stopped with that first one, and so hard and stiff and sudden that it near jarred the eye teeth out of that cowboy's head.

He was glad to let Scorpion stand for a few seconds. He wished that horse would go on a-bucking or do none at all, for these single hard jolts was not to his liking, and if he'd been just breaking the chestnut instead of wanting to save him for the long rides that was ahead he'd of been apt to run his thumbs along that bowed neck of his, give him his head and have it out with him.

But now was no time for such. So, as he pulled on the hackamore rein again this time he liked to jarred that pony's eye teeth out too, and before a kink come there was another pull on the hackamore rein, and another and another, until the horse was made to whirl in one direction and then another, giving him hardly no chance nor time to get his head down and go to bucking. When Tim let up on that, and while the chestnut was sort of dizzy by the whirling he lined him out straight ahead and sudden, and there was no more kinks in his back. Making sure of that he then rode him near to where Pete had been sitting, and getting off the chestnut there he stuck his hand out.

"Well, Pete old boy, I'll be riding on," he says, sort of quiet. "I'd of liked to stayed and kept you company while you're recuperating, and I could of took on the broncs where you left off, but it can't be done now. But I'll keep letting you know where I am from time to time and if you'll do the same we'll be riding together again some day. Do as you wish with my gray, he's yours now."

Pete couldn't say much. There was nothing much for him to say anyhow, only to wish Tim luck and warn him again of Scorpion and not trust him as he himself had.

"So long, Pete," says Tim as he rode by, "and take care of yourself"

"I still think he's only an ordinary bronc," Tim grinned; "only maybe kind of rough in spots, but that'll wear off after a couple of days' riding."

Scorpion hardly moved as Tim turned and got on him again, and as he was rode by Pete who was now leaning on the corral gate and holding it open his bowed neck was stretched out, his ears and nose pointed for the open country and his gait was at a distance eating walk.

"So long, Pete," says Tim as he rode by, "and take care of yourself. I'll be taking the south pass. So long."

"So long, Tim," answers Pete, "and be good. If you can't be good be careful, for you're an outlaw now and riding an outlaw."

That last warning sort of went home with Tim, and as he rode out thru the night he would be careful to remember and act according. Pete watched the shape of him and Scorpion blur into the dark, and when he couldn't see them no more he listened to the horse's hoofs on the hard trail for sounds of the horse acting up and busting loose, but the sounds of the hoof beats went on regular and steady as that with any good traveling horse.

Hearing them no more, Pete waited for a while and closed the corral gate, then taking his chair he hopped along the corral to where the gray was standing, took off the bridle that was still on his head, turned him in with the broncs and then opened another corral gate out to the pasture and watched 'em go by. Somehow he then of a sudden missed Scorpion. There was something about that horse he'd liked and he wished he'd had the chance of finding out what was back of his queer and sometimes mighty wicked acting. The horse sure wasn't "weedy" (locoed). If anything he showed plenty of brains by his good judgement as to when to fight, when to be docile, and how to get a man off his guard. Then again the horse sometimes acted as tho he was being governed by some power he had no say about, and that's what Pete would of liked to got to the bottom of.

In the hundreds of horses he'd handled he'd never run acrost such a horse, and he wished for that one reason that there'd been another good horse Tim could of took in the place of him. Another good reason was that Scorpion was not fit for a man on the dodge and who has to depend so much on his horse at such times, and even tho Tim was a top hand with broncs, Pete would be kind of worried until he heard from him.

But nothing else could of been done. And now that the plans had been changed sudden and Tim decided to ride out that night instead of waiting till the next day, the gray couldn't very well be taken out as had been planned and left to range with Pete's horses. For them horses would of been hard to find at night, specially by Tim who didn't know where they ranged. Besides it was best for Tim to waste no time that way right then.

Pete thought on the subject as with the help of his chair and stick he made his way back to the bunk house, and he thought of many other things as he eased out of his clothes, made it to his bunk and before he went to sleep.

It was a short while after daybreak the next morning when he got up and waited for the ranch hands to come to breakfast, and as they got thru eating he got one of 'em to corral the broncs, catch the gray horse and lead him out to where his horses was ranging and turn him loose with 'em, saying that the gray was a company horse that had strayed in somehow, and he didn't want him in the bronc pasture as there wasn't any too much feed there as it was.

But he didn't want him to get away, he says. He pointed to where his horses ranged, and seeing the ranch hand ride out and leading the gray a while later, Pete felt better and as tho Tim's trail had been wiped off the earth. A breeze which turned into a stiff wind came up along middle forenoon, too stiff a wind for Pete to be a-sitting under the big cottonwood, and as he went in the bunk house he felt still better, for Tim's trail of the night before would be blowed over or off altogether, and Tim was now riding a horse of another color.

Pete was relieved some more when as the afternoon drug on and then evening come no riders showed up on the trail. With any kind of luck Tim would now be at least fifty miles away. He would still have a whole night to go on and even tho Scorpion wasn't used or hardened in to packing a man a long ways, Pete figured that horse had the good age and strength to do it, and in one night and a day and another night, Tim, even with taking on good enough rests for himself and the horse, could easy enough be eighty or a hundred miles away by the next morning. That's a lot of country and distance when it's where automobiles can't go, and with the tracks blowed away even a blood hound couldn't of found which way to've led, or caught up if he could.

It was after supper and getting dark when Pete lit the lamp in the bunk house and went to reading some more on the newspapers of the evening before. The wind was still blowing strong outside, and as he settled himself down to comfortable reading he looked out the open door and says to that wind, "Let 'er rip, old boy, and let 'em come."

And like in answer to them words the wind got fiercer, then he heard the sound of hoofs on the hard road, soon the jingling of spurs, the creaking of saddle leather and four riders came to sight at the door of the bunk house.

CHAPTER SIX

SURPRISED but thinking fast, Pete had slipped the newspapers under his bunk at the first sounds of the horses' hoofs on the hard earth, and now he seemed plum at ease and looking at a magazine when one of the men got off his horse and came towards the open door. Pete then natural like looked his direction.

"Howdedo?" he says before the rider got to the door. "Come on in."

"Howdy?" says the rider, looking around the bunk house a bit and then at the crippled up Pete. "We've been riding hard and a long ways," he went on. "Could we get something to eat and a little hay and grain for our horses? There's four of us."

"Sure," says Pete. He pointed at the cook house. "You go over there and tell the Chink I said to give you 'big feed' and he'll fix you up. And while he's fixing that up take your horses to the stable. It's right by the road a little ways and there's a hay stack right by the stable. The grain is in a bin on the right hand side as you go in the door, and help yourself. I'd go along with you but I can't navigate very well. You won't need no help anyway."

The rider glanced at Pete's leg and foot. "Sure, we'll make out all right," he says. "What did you do, let a horse fall on you?"

"Yep," grinned Pete. "Fell on me while I was in the air."

"How long ago?"

"Going on a month now."

After the riders had gone, Pete got to thinking, "Well, they've come, sure enough," and mighty quick too. He wondered about the first rider not inquiring nor doing any investigating before wanting to put up the horses and getting food for himself and the others, but he come to figuring that some investigation might of already been done from outside, and that one or two men had come up afoot and seen him a-sitting by the lamp, all by his lonesome and unsuspecting.

He thought of the newspaper he'd been reading, and looking at the window he figured that on account of the high table he'd been sitting close to and the way he'd been holding the paper it would of been hard for anybody from the outside to tell whether he'd been reading a newspaper or magazine.

The bunk house and cook house had most likely been investigated too, from outside, quiet, and by men afoot before they got back on their horses and rode on in.

He was double glad now that the gray horse had been turned out on the range, and he hoped that the men hunters didn't get to talk to ranch hands and ask about that gray. But that didn't worry him so much, for the ranch hands wouldn't be apt to pay attention to the brand and description of the gray as a cowboy naturally would and they wouldn't be able to tell much, and being that Pete had said he was a company horse

One of the men got off his horse and came towards the open door

he'd be considered as such. There'd been many horses come and gone since Pete had come to the ranch, one of the many ranches of the Cross Bell outfit, and the ranch hands didn't get to pay much attention to 'em. When they did pay attention it wouldn't be to the brands nor marks. The pretty ones would be the only ones catching their eye, and the gray wasn't a horse a ranch hand would call pretty.

It was good, Pete thought, that neither of them, not even the Chink, had seen Tim. So he figured he wouldn't have to do much explaining to satisfy the men hunters.

Soon enough they came back from the stable, three of them, and the fourth from the cook house, and they walked in the bunk house to wait for the Chink's holler. They was big and tired looking men, and with all the guns and ammunition they had with 'em, near enough to furnish Villa's men for a small war, he wondered how come their horses had packed 'em this far. Tim had only his forty-five and a few rounds of ammunition.

Pete didn't know any of the men, and after his first howdy and telling 'em to make themselves comfortable he didn't speak unless he was spoke to, and he wasn't spoke to much, for two of the men had sort of took the floor with their lamenting about how sore and stiff they was from riding, how much skin they'd lost and how sore and stiff they'd be the next day. The other two didn't have no comments on that, they was just hungry, and Pete had figured at one glance of them that they'd seen many a long day in the saddle, with cattle, before they went to hunting men. One of 'em was talked to as the sheriff, the other deputized as a tracker, and Pete held them two responsible for having the other two on Tim's trail so quick. Them other two would of looked more fitting on cement, in alleys, raiding dives or in automobiles chasing gangsters on highways, they sure looked out of place and miserable where they was, and Pete figured they couldn't even catch cold in this country.

The Chink pounded on the wagon tire by the cook house and all filed out that direction. Pete would now have some time to himself and do some thinking. Him and Tim had sure figured about right as to when officers would be showing up at the soonest, and Pete was more than glad that Tim had decided to hit out the night before instead of waiting until the morning. Now he would have a good chance to get away even if the sheriff picked up his trail, which would be impossible.

He got up, and taking his chair along he found the newspapers which he'd hid under his bunk, went to the stove, stuck 'em in and lit a match to 'em. For being there was no other newspapers in the bunk house these late ones telling all about the train hold up would of looked sort of suspicious if found all by themselves, like to show that somebody there had been more than interested to reading about the hold up than general every day news.

The papers burnt down quick and without heating the stove, Pete mixed the black ashes with the old gray ashes that was already in the stove, dumped some little trash over 'em and he was satisfied. There was nothing else around the bunk house that would give any hint of Tim being there. Then hopping along outside he looked the direction of the ranch hands' bunk house for a light there. There seldom ever was in the summer, for the days being long it would be near time for the men there to hit the soogans when dark come. They'd be up at daybreak, and as usual no light showed from their bunk house that night.

Pete was again sitting in the same position and with the magazine on his lap, when he heard the screen door springs squeak. That squeak would of been a signal to him if one of the men had come out to watch what he'd do while the others et, and Pete had made sure they'd all went in before he started burning the papers and went to looking around.

Now, their appetites all satisfied, the four men came in the bunk house and went to stretching out on the bunks that was along the walls. All but the sheriff who, sitting on the edge of one bunk, started rolling a cigarette in a slow and thinking way.

Then having it rolled he looked up at Pete before lighting it and asked:

"Do you know if any of the Cross Bell men been to town lately, took a train east and then came back?"

"No," says Pete. "I wouldn't know. I've been only at this one ranch steady since early spring."

"Did anybody stop or ride by here the last few days?"

"No," says Pete again; "not for about two weeks

and that was one of the boys from the wagon who'd come to get the broncs I'd started." Then he thought sudden. Maybe they'd seen Tim's horse's tracks somewhere on their way and leading to the ranch, maybe close too. He didn't want the sheriff to think he was lying, so he says, "Come to think of it, there was a rider come by here. I think it was day before yesterday."

"Did he stop?"

"No."

"What kind of a horse was he riding?"

Pete had been prepared for these questions, and thinking that maybe Tim had been seen on the gray without his knowing and the sheriff had traced him this far on that clue he wasn't going to be caught lying this time either.

"He was riding a gray," he says, realizing that that would only help Tim, for now he was riding a dark chestnut.

At the word "gray" the three stretched out officers sat up and one of 'em says, "That's him."

Paying no attention, the sheriff went on to ask Pete, who had acted sort of surprised at the other officer's remark:

"What kind of a looking feller was riding the gray?"

"Well, I couldn't tell very well from where I was at the time. I was under the cottonwood outside here, but I couldn't help but notice how queer he looked on a horse, short and fat and humped over. Must of been an oldish man."

The officer who'd spoke up stretched himself back on the bunk with a disgusted grunt. "No, that's not him," he says.

"What kind of clothes was he wearing?" the sheriff asks Pete.

"Well, they was neither dark nor light. No special colors that I can remember, but from where I was I could tell he was wearing batwing chaps." Tim had been wearing "chinks" (Armitas) (a buckskin or light leather covering that ties or buckles around the waist and goes only below the knees).

"How big was the horse he was riding?" asks the sheriff, "and what color was his mane and tail?"

"He was riding a kind of small horse, about 900, I should judge, and his mane and tail was light." Tim's gray had a dark mane and tail, and a good sized horse, weighing around 1100.

"Did you get to see which way this rider came from and which way he went?"

"Not very much. When I first seen him he was on the road, like coming from town. You can't see much of that road from here, you know. But I seen him ride past the corrals, and on account of that strip of poplars there I couldn't see which way he went after that."

"Hum," says the sheriff, not giving any hint as to wether the information he got done him any good or not. Then after a while he asks.

"Do you know a man by the name of Jim Smith? He's described as a cowboy and his description fits you pretty well, age, size and all, but the cooky tells me, as you said, that you've been here since last spring and that you've been layed up for near a month, and that don't match with the man I'm after because that man was up and a-going strong just a few days ago, and a long ways from here."

"Well," grins Pete, "I guess it's a good thing I'm not just drifting thru and couldn't prove where I've been or I might be taken in for whatever that man Jim Smith done. . . . No. I don't know nobody by that name." And Pete felt truthful there, even tho he did have a heap more than a hunch as to who this Jim Smith was.

The sheriff then went to tell him the whole story of the train hold up as he got it, of the train robbers being robbed in turn by supposed to be four men. But the sheriff believed there'd been only one man, this Jim Smith, and he didn't believe that that one man killed the two guards, not the way that man had acted. He figured that Smith had just sort of fell in on the hold up, and like a reckless, happy go lucky cowboy, seen a lot of fun in scattering the hoodlums, taking the loot and their guns away from 'em and leaving 'em helpless and easy to catch.

The sheriff gave a hint that that cowboy had ought to have a medal, even if he did run off with the money. Maybe he figured on returning it. And now that the dangerous punks, dangerous thru their ignorance, cowardliness and want of notoriety, had been caught, was where they belonged, he felt that justice had been well done to the case, thanks to Smith, and that all should be well satisfied, for they'd got the crooks.

As for Smith, the sheriff gave Pete the hint that he wasn't so anxious to get him, but duty was duty, and there he was.

Now there was a $5000 reward for the capture of that man and the money is returned. "Such a reward is worth looking out for, and all you got to do to keep a good description of him in mind is look at yourself once in a while," the sheriff said as he ended.

Pete seemed very interested. "Wow," he says; "$5000 is a lot of money. That would start a feller out with a nice little bunch of cattle. I wish I could ride for it, and it's just my luck I can't. But maybe it's just as well I can't, I'd most likely be wasting time because I sure wouldn't know where to start looking for him. But I'll sure watch out and do my best from here."

There was snores from two of the bunks before Pete and the sheriff got thru talking. The sheriff grinned at the noise. "Well, I guess I'd better put these boys to bed."

The bunks was filled with wild hay, some of 'em topped off with a few old soogans (quilts). They'd do well for the tired men, and the night being warm there wouldn't be much need for covers, besides they'd be sleeping with most of their clothes on. But at least the boots should be pulled off, and cartridge belts unbuckled. The sheriff woke up the two officers and told 'em to do so and get comfortable as they could, for there'd be another big day tomorrow. The tracker had already made himself comfortable for that day and the sheriff soon followed suit.

Pete sat up for a little while, but being sort of kept on the jump that evening had tired him some, and when he hit for the soogans he soon was also asleep.

He woke up at daybreak, so did the sheriff, and as he heard him stir he layed still and waited for him to get up first. The other officers was still in full swing at their snoring, and Pete didn't think they'd turn over at all during the night, not even when they'd come near choking as they now was doing every so often and regular like.

Mumbling that he could sleep well alongside a bellering herd but not at all by this wood sawing and knot hitting contest, he sat up on his bunk and went to rolling a cigarette. Pete, grinning at the sheriff's remark, also begin to sit up. It was slow work for him and the sheriff came to his help and then the two went to smoking and talking.

The talk was of course about the robbery mostly but, to sort of rest his mind some from the duties that'd been bearing down on him lately, the sheriff's talk often switched to cattle, range, horses and old cowmen and riders he used to know and still knowed. That was fine by Pete, only he was careful not to mention any of the ranges and outfits where him and Tim rode together so he wouldn't be connected with him in any way in case it was found out that Jim Smith's true name was Tim Birney.

Pete had rode in many other countries, some where the sheriff had also rode and before he started riding for the law, and it was natural that the talk got to be

And then the two went to smoking and talking

mighty interesting to the sheriff, talking old times that way and with one who'd been there. It had got so interesting that the rip saw noises was hardly heard, and the sheriff didn't think of stirring his men and getting 'em up in time for breakfast.

The talk was cut short as the Chink hammered a tune on the wagon tire and the sheriff jumped to get his men up. The tracker jumped out of his bunk at about the same time but the other two, even tho they opened their eyes and tried to, could only groan and slump back to where they'd started. They was stiff and sore from the tips of their hair roots to the tips of their toe nails, they said, raw in places and their flesh stuck to their clothes. They didn't think they could make it.

The sheriff had to grin a little at the looks on their faces. "You'll be all right soon as you get up and wash and move around a bit," he says. Then to Pete, "I guess I been kind of hard on 'em," he went on; "they're not used to riding; in fact, have hardly ever been on a horse before and we rode at least sixty miles yesterday."

"Yeh, I guess it would be kind of tough on 'em all right," agrees Pete, "but what I'm wondering about most is how the horses stood it."

The ranch hands had got thru with their breakfast and was headed for the stable by the time the two officers had groaned themselves into their boots. The sheriff and the tracker had waited for them, then Pete noticing that the sheriff had seen the ranch hands and thinking that he'd most likely go out and speak to them, called 'em to the door and asked 'em if they would water and feed the horses in the stable.

"We already done that," says one of the men, "before we came to breakfast."

"Good," says the sheriff. Then he went on to ask 'em right there: "Did you boys see a rider come by here lately? He was riding a gray horse."

At the mention of the gray horse, Pete's heart liked to've turned over a few times and his eyes was hard on the man that had led him out and turned him loose. The ranch hands both looked at one another as much as to ask if either had seen such a rider lately. Finally (it seemed like an hour to Pete) one spoke up and said he hadn't seen no rider of any kind lately. The other one hadn't seen no rider either, but that he'd seen a loose gray horse. There was lots of gray horses, but——"

"Where?" asks the sheriff, quick, "and how long ago?"

"Down towards the flat here about a mile. He was all by his lonesome, and I guess that was about a week ago."

"You're sure it wasn't a couple or three days ago or since?"

"Yes. I'm sure it was about a week ago now, at least that."

"All right," says the sheriff, like to forget about the gray horse. "Now, about this man."

He pointed to the surprised Pete. "How long has he been working here?"

Both men shook their heads and both said they didn't

know, saying that he'd been at the ranch when they first come that spring.

"Has he been away from here for any length of time lately, say for two or three days?"

"No," they both said. He hadn't been away from the ranch no time since they'd been there, not even for a day.

"Well, I'm glad to hear that," says the sheriff, grinning, "but if you see a man of his description you boys had better glaum onto him if you can because such a man is wanted in connection with train robbery, and if you can ear him down until I can come and get him there'd be $5000 in it for you. That's the reward."

The ranch hands whistled in surprise as the sheriff turned away from 'em and they went on their way to the stables, and Pete drawed a long sigh of relief as he went to rolling a smoke.

"It's not that I doubted your word that I asked the boys the questions I did," says the sheriff to Pete. "It's that I was pretty sure that Jim Smith had come this way and they might of seen him when you couldn't. Now I'm sort of satisfied he didn't come this way. Most likely took to the north pass. The few tracks I seen now and again fooled me." He was quiet for a spell, then went on, like apologizing: "And as far as inquiring about you that's a matter of duty which I'm sworn in to do. I just wanted to make sure, even if I seen at a glance when I first walked in last night that the cast and them bandages on your foot and leg had been put on by a doctor and not as a bluff by yourself." He grinned again. "I could see by the color and wear on 'em that they'd been on quite a few days too."

"Well," says Pete, "I hope you're satisfied that I'm not Jim Smith now or I'll soon get to believing that I am."

The two stiffened up officers didn't get in on any of the conversation that morning, they was too busy on themselves, and finally getting washed up and with groans and grunts they buckled on their heavy cartridge belts and they stiff legged it behind the sheriff and the tracker to the cook house.

Pete had to feel a little sorry for them as he watched 'em. "They'll sure be good drags on the sheriff and the tracker," Pete thought as with his chair and stick he started for the corrals and stables. He wanted to be there to watch the officers leave, to see which direction they'd take and if the sheriff would get to talking to the ranch hands again. He also wanted to get a look at their horses.

He'd been at the stable quite a while, sitting in his chair and watching the tired horses eat. The ranch hands had hooked up their teams and gone to their work in the meadows when the four officers showed up, the sheriff and the tracker in the lead, and the two other officers, knock-kneed, and now walking bow-legged to keep their sore knees from rubbing together, was in the drags.

"Well," says the sheriff as he seen Pete at the stable door, "I see you can navigate some."

"Yes, some," grins Pete. "I was kind of curious to

With his chair and stick he started for the corrals and stables

see what kind of horses it took to pack them for a whole sixty miles in one day." He pointed at the two slow coming men.

The sun was up by the time the horses was saddled and the men was ready to go. All thanked him for his help towards their getting something to eat and a place to rest. Then the sheriff, getting on his horse, spoke up.

"And the horses thank you for a good bellyful and rest too," he says. "So long, and watch out for that five thousand."

With that, him and the tracker took the lead and the other two officers groaned their way along behind.

"Five thousand dollars," Pete said and repeated to himself as he watched the men ride away. Then he snorted a grin. "Why," he went on talking to space after 'em, "if I was a mind to pull a trick like that I know where I could find that box with twenty-four thousand in it, and without turning Tim in."

With the help of his chair and stick, he pegged his way out of the corral, went along the road a short ways and past the narrow strip of tall poplars, then clambering up a knoll and to where he could well see the valley below, he sat down to earth under the shade of a twisted juniper.

From there he could see well across the valley, fifteen miles to the range of hills bordering the other side, and now a couple of miles below him he could see the four officers a winding their way thru the sage to the valley and, as the sheriff had said, headed for the north pass.

On leaving town the sheriff had no idea as to which direction "Smith" had taken. None of the cowfolks had seen him along the way and there'd been no trace of him anywhere, so, on account of it being the most open country, he figured that the direction of the Cross Bell range would be the most likely country he'd hit for. Then a few miles from the ranch where Pete was he'd seen the first tracks of what he thought might well been made by Smith's horse. But the strong wind had blowed all signs of them away before he got to the ranch.

Then finding no lead of any kind at the ranch, he would just have to go on blind again and figure out another most likely country Smith would hit for. That would be the country to the north, beyond the north pass and where ranches was the furtherest apart, where it was less likely to be seen and a wanted man could hide out well, so it was natural that the sheriff decided on that direction.

That was one reason, as Tim had figured out, that he would take just the opposite direction, to the south and beyond the south pass. There would be a couple of thickly settled strips he'd have to go thru in that direction but he could pass them at night, skirt the towns, and then there'd be hundreds of miles where there wouldn't be even a drift or line fence to check him on his way to the country of wild horses and few people. People of the kind that had heard of telephones and fast trains on steel roads but had never seen neither.

In contrast of the day before, the air was still as

Pete sat in the shade of the juniper and watched the four officers ride on out of his sight. When he couldn't see them no more he could tell of their location some fifteen miles away by the tall soaring of the dust their horses stirred. It was middle forenoon when the dust couldn't be seen no more, then Pete got up, and looking towards the north pass once more he grinned at the still distance and remarked, "The hunters and the hunted are fast getting further apart, and every step Scorpion takes now means two." Then he started back for the stable where he would putter around some, look his rigging and outfit over for needed fixing up or improving. Maybe later he would go to the blacksmith shop and forge out a pair of spurs or a bit which he'd had in mind of making for a long time.

CHAPTER SEVEN

UNDER a lattice work of ocatilla stems grown over with wild grapevine and which made a cool and cheerful shade of green was a living picture of the kind that would make any desert weary rider pass up a last water hole in his hurry to reach and see.

The shade was to the north side of a small dobie ranch house and overlooking a deep canyon at the bottom of which a narrow ribbon of water could be seen a-winding thru. To the forked piñon timber supporting the shade hung a gunny sack covered earthen gourd of water and to one side of it was the brown head of a girl bent over a book and reading out loud. She was sitting on a regular boughten chair, her bright colored dress was ready boughten too and she made a pretty picture there under the green vines and gourd, in the cool shade on the hard packed dobie earth.

That's about as far as the interest of a weary desert rider would go, for beside the girl and also in the cool and comfortable shade, that space was already taken up. A man was stretched out on a cot there, and with the peaceful and contented look on his face had layed claim to that space.

But he'd been no weary rider when he first come and layed claim to that space, and he hadn't come there on his own will and power. He'd been out, out of his head and packed there, and after what all he'd gone thru it

A man was stretched out on a cot there

would seem like he was sort of entitled to first claim to that space of rest and peace and content.

That man was very thankful to fate, thankful for her using his horse to lay him down near such a paradise spot as he was now enjoying. He couldn't of thought nor hoped of ever finding such a place on earth and he'd of rode on by altogether missing the haven when fate, thru the horse he was riding, took a hand and stopped him there.

Jerry Nelson had got off his horse, a ganted up, leg weary and sore footed chestnut with slim bowed neck and Roman nose, watered him at a little spring that only run a few feet which sunk in the dry wash and then led him up the side of a hill and hobbled him there to graze and rest during the heat of the day. At first and when leaving the ranges away to the north the cowboy had rode at night and rested his horse in day time the way he was now doing, but it had been for precaution then and so he wouldn't be seen by any other riders, wandering sheepherders, or automobile drivers when having to go thru thickly settled places. After he'd passed all such places he then kept on riding nights, still for precaution and also because it was easier on his horse. He'd kept that up for over three weeks, and now, about a thousand miles south of the northern ranges where he'd started and at last in the country where he'd figured to hang out for a long spell he was still riding nights and looked around between sleeps during the day, during sunups and sundowns and while he et. Looking around for a hide out place where there would be a good spring and wild horses, antelope and lions come to water there. He'd have to have company of some kind besides his chestnut while he hibernated until things cooled down from them happenings to the north.

The cowboy knowed this country, he'd run mustangs in it some years before. It was a big country, and a few of the very few people that was in it also knowed him. By name he was known as Jerry Nelson there, just another name for Tim Birney, alias Jim Smith and other aliases. For Tim had formed the habit of changing his name in different countries, just for precaution and in case, and not on account that he intended to put a blemish on any name he took, but a feller gets into things once in a while that he don't expect to, like with that train hold up to the north for instance.

But he hadn't seen no use to changing the name of the chestnut that was now grazing in scattered tufts of bunch grass up on the side of the hill above the spring. That chestnut's name was still Scorpion, and only him and Pete Leon knowed him by that name, and a scorpion he'd showed himself to be many times along the thousand mile stretch and since leaving the Cross Bell corral. But he'd also proved himself a mighty good horse, a natural drifter that never seemed to tire, even if he did act like it once in a while. He more than surprised Tim that he could stand the ride he did, and even tho he was given all the chances and rests possible it would of took a mighty good and hardened horse used to packing a man to've followed him. As Pete had said, he was of good age, he had the nerve and wouldn't wear himself out fighting while traveling. While handling him from the ground was when he'd need watching, and Tim had found that out plenty well.

Tim had changed the Cross Bell brand on Scorpion's hide into Lazy B. H. Box, a kind of complicated iron and the bell had to be blotched some, but the original brand was pretty well disfigured and would be hard to trace or suspected of being there unless a feller had been present while Tim done the changing.

After hobbling his horse on feed that morning, Tim had as usual looked at the country around him. It was a sort of flat country of white sage, ocatilla, joshua and dagger with deep arroyos cutting thru it here and there and little mesa buttes jutting up and scattering. A hundred miles to the east of him, Tim could see a tall range of mountains. But only a couple of miles from him and in that same direction he couldn't see the half a mile deep and mile wide cut, the canyon which he'd of missed entirely if fate hadn't took a hand.

He'd cooked a breakfast of jack rabbit on coals that morning, one he'd knocked over with a rock the evening before, then his appetite being sort of satisfied he'd left the spring, went up the hill to near where Scorpion was grazing and went to sleep on the warm ground by a little shade of the taller sage.

He'd woke up during the middle of that afternoon, et the rest of the rabbit, and figuring on getting more meat he thought of riding along a bit during the light of day. He'd seen little bunches of antelope now and again during mornings and evenings of the last few days, and he figured that one of them would sure be

Tim had changed the Cross Bell brand on Scorpion's hide into Lazy B. H. Box, a kind of complicated iron and the bell had to be blotched some

worth one of his cartridges. He'd been mighty saving on the little ammunition he'd had, and for two good reasons, one was that it would be some time before he'd want to take a chance of showing himself to buy some, and the other reason was that the report of his .45 would reach a long ways and attract more attention than anything else in any country. But here, at last in the country he'd rode so hard to get to and where he figured on locating for a long spell, he felt safe in firing a shot even if it might be heard by somebody, for that somebody wouldn't have heard nor maybe never hear of that robbery away to the north, and wouldn't connect him with it if it had been heard of. But at the looks of the country around, Tim felt as tho he was the first one there. He'd never been in that perticular part of that country before. It looked mighty good to him, and he didn't think there was a human soul to within fifty miles to hear a shot if he fired one or ten.

And now, with getting an antelope, he could lay off near some spring for a day or so, jerk (dry) the meat and that would make a light pack that would last him a long time, until he could find a spot to his liking in around that country.

Thru with the last of the rabbit, Tim had went and got the chestnut which by then had had his fill and been resting. Scorpion had acted more tired and leg weary than usual that day. He'd acted that way before, and Tim had near been fooled enough to be careless at such times, but with the scary goings on that had followed such spells now and again, Tim had got to well remember Pete's warnings, and he'd felt lucky to've had a head left to remember with after each happening.

But he'd had antelope on the brain that day, and his eyes had been more at the country around for signs of some than on the mild and tired acting chestnut he'd been saddling. . . . Consequences was that the scorpion and devil showed up sudden and just as Tim pulled on the latigo to cinch up his saddle. Bared teeth caught him along the left short ribs, a hard knee followed up and caught him under the chin, and as everything went blank and dark for Tim the horse went on by and clipped him on the right shoulder with a hind hoof as he went and Tim was layed out flat on his back in the trickle of water by the spring.

Scorpion had gone on a-tearing and a-bucking in another one of his mad sprees, and as Tim hadn't got to finish the cinching the saddle soon loosened, got down to the horse's side, then under his belly and it was soon kicked off to lay not far away. The horse then, only a hackamore on his head, no bit in his mouth, raised his head and tail, and like an unbroke mustang of that country hit out acrost the flat on a wild run, mecate rope a-flying and like the devil was after him.

It had been a couple of hours later when old Joshua and his son Jake, a boy of about sixteen, came onto the saddle and then found Tim sprawled out below the spring. They'd been out all day, to see how the mustangs was running and fixing up an old water trap which they hadn't used for a long time. On their way back to the ranch they'd rode by the little spring for a drink and there Tim was, soaking up some of the water that trickled out.

That trickle of water had made him come to a couple of times and he'd sat up and looked around, but that had been as far as he'd got, for a pain that caught him in the pit of his stomach would lay him down again.

Scorpion had gone on a-tearing and a-bucking in another one of his mad sprees

He'd been unconscious when the two riders found him, and with Jake's help, Joshua packed him on his horse in as easy way as was possible and both holding him in place on each side took him on into the ranch, only a couple of miles away and below the rim of the canyon which Tim hadn't been able to see.

Once at the ranch everybody set to. Joshua and Jake took an arm each and Joshua's wife and grown daughter took the legs and packed Tim to the cot under the vine shade. Even the little daughter had took a hand and packed Tim's six shooter and cartridge belt.

Having had considerable practice patching up wounds and bones on members of her own family as well as members of other families, also on horses, cattle, goats, and chickens, Joshua's wife, Ophelia, went at Tim with experienced hands. It was no first hand treatment, and when she'd get thru and he would be healed up he'd be fit to stand as much punishment as before.

All accounted for, there'd been one broken collar bone, one cracked shoulder blade, two cracked ribs with some flesh and hide tore off by the side of them. The pains in the pit of the stomach had been caused by them hurts, and a rock as he'd fell.

Tim had come to while Ophelia was still working on him and his first glimpse had been of the daughter, Jane, who was bending over him and helping her mother at tightening a wide bandage around his shoulder and over his collar bone. He'd been for sitting up at the first sight of the pretty head bending over him but the mother held him back, told him that all was fine and to lay still.

He layed still for near a week, and after the first night and the next day he got to minding the laying less and less. For it seemed like he'd dropped, or been pounded and kicked, into a home heaven. All took turns in taking care of him and do what they could for him, and of evenings when all gathered for after supper rests and talks, he was most always made the center of the gathering. For Tim had been around and seen the outside world. He'd been as far east as Chicago a few times, down into Mexico and all thru the western states up into Canada. He could talk of many strange and interesting things, people and places, besides he knowed stock and range. They'd heard of and remembered the name Jerry Nelson. They'd heard of his skill and nerve at riding, roping and mustang running, and that name had spread in that country and was still mentioned when some bad horse was talked of.

On account of them hearing of him that way was maybe the reason why they hadn't wondered how he come to be in their barren country where few but wild horse and lion hunters like Joshua ever stayed. It took a heap of territory to support a family or even one man in that land, more than it would take to support a big town in other lands. It wasn't a country that would attract or keep any ambitious man for long unless he was born and raised there, like Joshua, or was on the dodge and wanted to hide out. But if Joshua and his family wondered or suspicioned anything as to his being there, Tim thought they done a fine job hiding it and they sure didn't seem to be worrying any on the subject.

The boy, Jake, seemed the most interested in Tim and was near him as long and often as he could, asking questions of the outside countries, the people, horses, cattle and such, never about towns. The grown girl, Jane, was a close second to Jake that way and the reason she wasn't first was because she was more spooky about asking the questions she wanted to ask. Towns wasn't for her either, but she did like to know the customs and ways of other people, how they dressed and what all they done.

Being she was at home pretty well all day, excepting sometimes when she'd go riding with her dad and brother to help bring in and corral a bunch of snaky horses, and helping her mother with the house and garden and other works, she had good excuses to be near and talk to him. If she didn't she'd sometimes make some, it all depended on how anxious she'd be to know about something she'd be wondering about, and as she popped on him that way and kept him company when her work was done for a spell, a grin of pity would sometimes come to Tim's face as he thought of poor old Pete (going on thirty years old) away to the north, layed up too and otherwise full of vim, wit and vigor, all by his lonesome excepting for the Chink cook and the two ranch hands, which was no company to him. And there Tim was, with all the good and cheerful company he could wish for in this desert land of plenty. He could spare some and wished Pete was with him to share it. They could be mighty good company to one another too, both being layed up the way they was, and they'd have plenty to talk about, also about Scorpion which now had the credit of flattening two good men and laying 'em side by side.

Tim often thought of writing to Pete and telling him to drift on down when he could, that here would be a good country to winter in, but he also thought that it would be best to wait a spell, for a letter from this far away range to a cowboy of the Cross Bell might be suspicioned and opened, more so that Pete hardly ever received any letters, and the little post office at the neighboring ranch might get curious. So he would wait until the smoke of the hold up sort of cleared and the smell evaporated. Then Pete would be able to travel. Besides it might be a long time before he would have a chance to get a letter mailed, maybe a couple of months. He might write Pete then.

It was sixty miles to the nearest post office and trading post, thru a dry country of no roads, only wild horse trails, and it was a hundred and sixty miles in that same direction to the nearest railroad, and about the only time Joshua ever went to the trading post or railroad was when he'd caught enough wild horses and figured the prices would make it worth while taking 'em in to the railroad and sell to buyers there, then he'd return with four or five horses loaded with grub, clothing, and whatever he could get for his good wife and family.

About the only time Joshua ever went to the trading post or railroad was when he'd caught enough wild horses and figured the prices would make it worth while taking 'em in

He'd sometimes take in mountain lion skins too and collect on the heavy bounty they brought, then sell the skins. In early spring he'd also take in cayote and lynx pelts which most always brought fair prices, and that way, Joshua provided for his happy family.

Jake had went along with him on them trips of marketing the "crops" of wild horses, furs and lion skins ever since he was ten years old, and Jane being a few years older had went before that. Sometimes she'd missed a few trips but as she'd got to growing up she got to wanting more things and hardly missed a trip from her fourteenth birthday on. She was now eighteen, to her full height of five foot three and good travelling weight of a hundred and twenty pounds, light on a horse, and she hadn't missed a trip to the trading post nor railroad the last two years.

It wasn't so much the sight of pretty clothes and such things that attracted her to the town by the railroad. She of course admired 'em and sort of wished she could have some, but that was in the same way with her as it would be with a mustang runner looking at a racy and shiny automobile. He'd like to have it too but it'd be of less use to him than a bottomless skillet. That was the way with Jane and the pretty party dresses. But she enjoyed going thru the store, looking at things and hearing strange jabbering as she went along, then she would get one or two house dresses, and as her and her mother wore the same size they would do for either and could be patterned from for more dresses of the different materials she'd get. Then there'd be some ornaments and nicknacks, socks, underwear, threads, needles, pins, and so on, also of course some candy for the "baby," little Margie, now eight years old, who still looked forward to her pretty colored candy on the return of every trip, regardless if she did get some better candy made at home once in a while, and it'd be a sort of sad happening if no town candy was brought her on the return of every trip.

Of evenings in town Jane and Jake would take on some picture show and enjoy it wether it was any good or not, for even tho the goings might not be interesting sometimes the costumes and settings would sort of make up for that.

A couple of soda pops or ice cream after the show and that would near end a day in town. Jane would go to her room in the hotel and look out the window to the street below, where if it would be Saturday nights or dance nights she would see and hear a lot of giddy goings on and remarks that sort of disgusted her and soon tired her of hotel rooms and town. A couple of nights and a day and she'd be ready and anxious to hit out early of mornings and breathe good desert air while astride a good horse and heading for home, fed up enough with town to last her for months and until time for another trip. It would be as a sort of a break like from sweet to sour pickles.

Jake didn't let the short spell in town affect him as it did Jane. He took it all in with a grin and missed nothing if he could help it. Boots shined, new overalls or cleaned pants, white shirt and black tie and little

Dakota hat cocked some to one side he felt as well dressed and fit to show himself as any man in that town. So, after leaving Jane at the hotel room, he'd prance out again, meander around some and then finally wind up to the hotel bar-room where his dad would most always be sitting at a table, taking on sociable drinks and talking horse with a few traders, buyers and mustang runners until Jake would show up. The last two years and since Jake got to meandering more and more by himself he got to showing up a little later each time, but most always, Joshua would be waiting in the bar-room for him and then the two would climb the stairs to their beds and rest. Jane in the room adjoining would pound on the door the next morning and wake 'em up.

With her trips to the town, Jane's shopping bundles put all together would seldom fill more than one "kyak" (rawhide covered pack box), but the bundles wasn't all clothing, dresses and such like. There would be school and other educational books and magazines, and newspapers and catalogs, also writing tablets and pencils. Plenty of reading and writing material for months and until another trip to town or trading post was made.

There'd been no schools for Joshua Bernard's children, and for good enough reasons, Joshua thought. The main one was that he couldn't afford to have his children stay in town, in a good enough place and furnish 'em with good enough clothes during that time. The closest school was at the trading post and there was no place where they could board there. But their mother, Ophelia, had had a good education, and with the school books and all kinds of good reading matter he didn't see where she couldn't turn 'em out as well educated and mannered as the average, maybe a whole lot more, for the desert would sure do its share in teaching 'em many things that would stand 'em good any place. They'd be far from helpless, and even tho they might never learn where the Isle of Capri might be, they'd know their own U. S. A. and easy enough fall into the ways of any part of it in case they left their home territory.

Ophelia more than agreed with her husband. For one thing she didn't want to part with her children for no length of time, and she couldn't of stood living in town till school was over even if it could be afforded, and with their going alone she was afraid of what they would learn that wasn't in school books. So she teached Jane to the best of her knowledge and kept on with all that was educational. Jane, in turn, and with the coaching of her mother teached Jake till he figured he was educated enough, then she started on little Margie who was plenty ornery at times but she learned fast and could now read and understand many books and magazines that she picked on.

All said and done Joshua's happy little family was all well educated as them who lived next door to schools. They wasn't much educated in the ways of towns but the good clean ways of the desert more than made up for that. Towns are easy enough to get educated to, for there's plenty of noises and talk. But the desert is mighty silent, gives no signs nor warnings and it takes a long time to know it.

* * *

Joshua's wife, Ophelia, hadn't been much for going along to town, not since the children come, and now she was very satisfied to just hear about it and read some of the goings on in the outside world when her family would return home.

Joshua had got a buckboard for her so she could drive to the trading post or town and back along with the trips while the children was small. But on account of the many deep arroyos that cut up the land, some of 'em forty feet acrost, near as deep and with straight up and down banks it was impossible to get that buckboard any closer than thirty miles to the ranch, not unless many bridges was built or steep cuts was made, and Joshua sure wasn't equipped with the material or time to do any such work.

So the buckboard was left in a shelter as close to the ranch as it could be got without having to take it apart, and if Ophelia would decide or need to go to town she would have to ride the thirty miles to it. A team would be harnessed and led over, hooked onto the buckboard and she or Joshua could drive on from there, letting Jane or Jake bring the two saddle horses on to the trading post.

Ophelia hadn't been to town for near three years, and she thought now that with Tim being on the ranch to do the few chores, such as milking a couple of cows, feeding a few hogs and the chickens, she could go along with that fall trip when Joshua would have a couple of carloads of mustangs to sell. He figured on averaging five dollars a head on the wild ones that year.

There would be a few lion skins to collect bounties on too, and being the cayote and lynx pelts had brought good prices the winter before, Ophelia had sort of planned on a good Christmas celebration, getting some presents for the whole family, nuts and candies and hide 'em until that time, then bake a lot of cakes and cookies, and with a couple of wild turkeys to decorate the platter there'd be real doings on that coming Christmas.

That would of course all depend on Tim staying until she could get to town and back. He'd be up and healed enough to take care of the chores by then, and if he would stay and do that she could go. If not it would be all off. For neither Jake nor Jane could be spared to stay behind because it took all three of 'em, Joshua, Jane, and Jake, to hold the wild ones together as they was started out of the pasture where they'd been held. It would be ticklish work driving the mustangs for about three days or until they was past their range.

So, telling Joshua of her plans one day, Ophelia and him came to Tim while Jane and Jake and Margie was away exploring a new found cave by the side of the canyon wall. Tim was stretched out, reading and seeming very much at peace, and as he seen by their faces that they was about to ask him something he perked up some more.

There would be a few lion skins to collect bounties on too

The cheerful look on his face made it easy for Joshua to come to the subject on his mind, and after he got thru spreading his wife's plans that only added one more spark to Tim's twinkling eyes.

"Why sure," he says after Joshua got about thru. "I'd be glad and feel mighty privileged to hold down the outfit while you folks are gone, and if it's not to be for another month or two why I'll be in fighting shape by then, with this care I'm getting."

Then, mighty pleased and with a hopeful look in her eyes, Ophelia asked him:

"Could you stay until Christmas and then spend the holidays with us? We'd sure be glad to have you."

"Well," says Tim, surprised. "That would sure be fine, but I'm afraid that's taking a lot of advantage of your good hospitality. But if I can be of any use and can make a hand of myself in any way I'd sure be glad to accept your invitation."

"You'd be making a hand of yourself by just staying," says Joshua.

"All right," grins Tim. "But if you find me missing a while after you get back from town you'll know the reason why."

"Jake and my husband are pretty good trackers," says Ophelia, smiling; then she turned and went back into the house.

That being settled, Ophelia happily went on making more plans, some she hadn't dared make before for fear they would be spoiled by Tim having to leave. But if she made plans, Tim also went to work on some of his own. He hadn't enjoyed nor celebrated a Christmas for many years, not since he left his Idaho home, and from then on that day had most always come and gone without even his knowing. It had been just another day.

For Tim had no home. His parents had died before he was Jake's age, he'd been fifteen. His only sister married and Tim left the home grounds forever, with only two saddle horses and his outfit, and leaving the home and little ranch to his sister, he went out on his own in the big country.

Now he was closer to his own home and kind than ever since he started rambling, and he felt the memories of his own home and folks coming back to life at its happiest times, before the old folks went so soon. He would now also plan, like Ophelia planned hers, for a Christmas that would set him back to some fifteen years.

With that in his mind and all pleasant scheming for that day, for the days between and the days after, it was no wonder there now was peaceful and contented looks on Tim's face as he star gazed up the green vine shade and Jane would come and read to him or just sit and talk. He felt mighty privileged and obligated in occupying such a space, not only in the cool shade but in the hearts of such people.

CHAPTER EIGHT

IT had taken a lot of persuading and a little more to keep Tim to his cot for the first week after his accident, then he'd done it a lot more to please Ophelia than himself. He'd took his medecine grinning, even to being tucked in and tied down with the tarp for the night, for, as she'd said, there always was a fever with such hurts as he had, and the quieter he layed and the warmer he was the sooner he'd get well. The nights would be plenty cool along the edge of the canyon, and Tim didn't want to go inside. Couldn't get used to that, he'd said.

Grinning at Ophelia's and Jane's concerned looks, he'd sat up at the end of the first week. But if he got any satisfaction out of sitting up he didn't get any more comfort, for, fearing he might try to use his right arm which might do a lot of damage with the knitting of the shoulder blade and collar bone, Ophelia bandaged his whole arm and hand all the tighter on his short ribs too, and as she got thru with that she backed off with a daring sort of laugh, and like she was talking to a tied down ornery bronc she says, "Now do your darndest, durn you." Jane had to laugh with her at the cornered and helpless look on Tim's face. Then he had to grin too.

"All right," he says, looking down at his buried right hand and then up at Jane. "All right, now you've got yourself into something too. You've got to roll cigarettes for me, and I smoke a lot of 'em. So you better start in right now because I need one after all this."

"But I don't know how to roll cigarettes," Jane laughed, "or can't you roll them with one hand? I've read of wild, rooting, tooting, shooting cowboys doing that."

"Well, I'm not that kind you generally read about," grins Tim. "I'm just the old fashioned breed. Besides it'd be mighty hard to do with a left hand. So you'd better get yourself a pan so's to catch all the tobacco you spill and start to practising. When your mother turns me loose again I'll relieve you of that job."

So that kind of evened things for Tim as trussed up like a mummy he sat up in the shade and watched Jane at her first tries at rolling a cigarette, and the pleasure he'd got at watching and coaching her well made up for his not being able to use his right hand for a spell.

An hour or so of practising and Jane finally built a cigarette that could be smoked at for a few puffs. It was fat in the middle and poor at both ends, and after the few puffs it split open, the tobacco spilt out and that was the end of that cigarette.

But she got a few rolled that Tim could sort of smooth over with his left hand and get enough puffs out of to sort of tide him over, and with a little more practice that evening as all gathered around as usual she got to rolling a pretty fair cigarette, better every day from then on.

Tim sure liked to watch her as she'd sit acrost from

Ophelia bandaged his whole arm and
hand all the tighter on his short ribs

him, a pan on her lap and rolling cigarette after cigarette. She would roll about a dozen at a spell and lay 'em in a saucer on a table there, and it would take her quite a while, specially at first, to roll that many cigarettes, for trying to make them as best as she could she would roll some over and over again until she was satisfied she couldn't do no better for the time.

As he watched her nimble fingers, Tim got to noticing that she had mighty pretty hands, small, well-shaped and not showing their strength. Then his eyes often went to her face, and watching the different expressions there as she was so intent to twisting cigarettes and making do as she wanted 'em to he thought she had a mighty pretty set of features, smooth, regular and sure expressive, and once in a while as she'd look up sudden and laugh at some misslip she'd make in rolling a cigarette he got to noticing them deep blue eyes of hers, deep as they was blue and like lighting her whole being, showing not a flaw in heart, spirit and body.

"A desert flower, the prettiest of flowers, and this one can't be pictured," says Tim to himself one day as he seen her standing in the doorway and smiling at him. "What a woman she'd make a good man!"

"A good man," he then thought, "don't mean a man on the dodge."

The realizing of that hit Tim kind of sudden and when Joshua and Jake rode in that evening and all gathered around after the supper was over he was quiet and even sad like. But that wasn't for long, for Joshua had news for him which stirred him out of that trance like as if he'd sudden found use of his right arm.

"I seen that chestnut of yours today," Joshua had said. "He's running with a wild bunch we've been trying to get for a long time, and he's as wild as the rest of 'em, if not wilder."

"Sure it was him?" asks Tim, all alive.

"Why, no mistaking. I got up to within a few hundred yards of the bunch he was in before they got wind of me, and by your description of that horse it was him all right. He still has the hackamore on his head and the rope was wore short to it and all frazzled out."

Tim come near tugging to get his arm free and getting to riding after him at the news, and at his show of excitement the family had to smile some. But he soon cooled down and he then smiled too, with pleasure that the horse was in the country. He'd often thought of him and the fear of losing him made him feel bad at times. But now that he'd been seen after these few weeks and was running with a wild bunch proved that he'd located in the country and that was great news to Tim. He'd get well soon now and then he'd have Scorpion again after that, he figured.

But the getting well didn't come along near so fast as Tim expected or wanted. It was a week from the time he'd heard of Scorpion being in the country before Ophelia finally left the bandages so just his right hand from the wrist was freed. That of course let Jane out of the cigarette rolling job and that was the only thing Tim was sorry for.

He still has the hackamore on his head and the rope was wore short to it

Being now that he'd been up and around for some time he tried to be of some help but there was nothing he could do. He couldn't even lift a bucket on account of his side, besides Ophelia wouldn't let him, nor even let him try to dry the dishes, saying that Jane and little Margie was well able to do that. So he just sort of walked around and kept the lady folks company from kitchen to garden, stables and chicken coops.

There was something he could use that poor old Pete to the north couldn't and that was his legs. So when he wasn't ambling along with Joshua and Jake and strutting around the corrals with 'em as they worked he was along with Jane. He was along with Jane more than with any of the others, she was outside more, but that wasn't the only reason. He of course pestered Ophelia once in a while and even strutted with little Margie now and again.

That little kid was sure smart, he thought, but sometimes she was a sort of a nuisance, when she stuck around as him and Jane was puttering around and talking, and sometimes she'd pass remarks at the table about him and Jane that would make the family grin or laugh but sure made him and Jane feel mighty uncomfortable and to blushing to the hair roots.

One day as she came along while Tim was near the corrals and stargazing down the blue of the deep canyon and the two got to talking he blurts out and asks her:

"Has sister Jane got any beaux?"

Little Margie wrinkled her nose and laughed. "Oh,

yes," she says, "lots of 'em, but Pappy don't seem to like any of 'em. He calls 'em names and they don't ride in here much."

Tim grinned. "Well," he says, "how does Jane feel about it, would she like to have them come?"

Little Margie shrugged her shoulders. "I don't know," she says. "I've never seen her cry or feel bad when Pappy would say things to her about 'em."

"How do you know she didn't when you wasn't looking?"

Little Margie giggled. "But I'm most always looking, and I sleep with her, you know." She was quiet for a spell and went on: "She did have a beau once I think she liked quite a bit. She met him at the Trading Post, but she told me he couldn't come to see her on account he couldn't drive his car any closer than forty miles to here. He was a man who went around the country selling things and she wrote to him a few times. She got a lot of letters from him, but I think he's gone down the wash now too."

"What do you mean?"

"Well, she's not writing to him any more."

Little Margie went on to tell a lot of things of interest that way to Tim, of interest because right at the time there didn't seem to be anybody on Jane's trail, and even tho he wondered why he should be interested and feel glad about it, he was glad about it anyhow and he soon quit wondering.

With different little talks that way it came to Tim

one day that if he got little Margie's confidence she'd be of mighty good use to him in a plan of his which he'd been fretting about putting thru without any of the rest of the family knowing. So, testing her and finding her true he told her of his plan and for her to gather up all the latest mail order catalogs she could find, some paper, envelopes, stamps, and a pencil, and making it a secret with her and telling how important it was she felt mighty big and pleased to be in cahoots with Tim on such a big secret. No hot iron could of made her tell on her "pardner" in the deed that was to be performed.

Picking her time, and while Jane and her mother was outside, working in the garden or doing some odd chores, she would sneak in the house, get a latest mail order catalog, just one at a time for fear they'd be missed, and then hightail to where Tim would be waiting, below the round corral and where Jane and her mother never went. There the two would go thru the catalog together and when one was gone thru it was taken back and another was brought out, the writing paper, envelopes and stamps was smuggled out a piece or two at the time and in the same way.

This went on for days, and the only fear Tim had of any give away was how little Margie acted when the family gathered at the house. She would feel her importance in her secret and act mysterious, too mysterious, and the folks got to noticing it, even to asking her what was the matter with her and her ways of acting, but to that she'd only act blank or maybe giggle a neutral answer. Tim was afraid that Jane or her mother would make her tell.

He warned her about that, she promised she would never tell and the two went on to work on their plot. But first tho, thought Tim, and to bind things, it would be wise to make his plotting pardner feel sure of a reward for her share in the deal and so she'd keep her secret. So, as they went thru catalog after catalog and as she put a finger down on an object she wanted he would write it down for order. There was so many things she wanted, things she'd been wanting "all her life" as she'd say, and so Tim would mark down everything.

Only thing was, after all was summed up there seemed to be an over amount of one thing, and that was dolls, a whole family of ten of 'em and from sizes as big as herself on down.

"Yes," Tim remarked to that; "you sure want a whole family to start with, don't you?"

One look at her and there was no doubt but what she did, so the order stood. There was other things such as little cast-iron stoves, skillets, furniture, and etc., etc. It took a long page for her order alone and nothing was checked off.

"You must remember one thing, young lady," Tim says, after she was finally satisfied, "and that is that all this stuff will have to be packed on horses and you've near got two pack horse loads in this list now."

"Oh, we have lots of horses," was all she said to that.

Tim grinned. "All right," he says; "but with the other stuff we've got to get for the others, why it's going to take some more horses. . . . Now," he went on, "you didn't pick out any dresses or shoes or bonnets or any thing like that. Don't you want a few? That wouldn't weigh much."

She'd never thought of such, but after considering a spell she picked out an assortment of them "necessary" things.

This all was of course a Christmas order being made out and according to Tim's plans. And now that little Margie was satisfied she was held to her word to help and keep all a secret by the fact that the order could be tore up if she didn't. But that wasn't necessary, for the importance of the secret alone was enough to keep her to it.

With her help, and thru her way of finding out and knowing, Tim got to know exactly what Ophelia and Jane would like to have and been wanting for a long time. Things for the house, for bureaus, and even to measurements for dresses and what kind. There was only one thing Tim figured couldn't be got to the ranch very well and that was a piano, but he'd see Joshua about that.

The ladies' list was pretty long, longer than little Margie's, but that was finally done satisfactory to the two plotters. Then there would be the list for Joshua and Jake, and outside of a suggestion or two, little Margie wasn't much help there, for Tim had a good idea of what they would like the most.

All set and done and sealed, little Margie was now done with her secretive work. All she'd have to do now would be to keep the secret, and as the days dragged on, that was getting to be harder and harder for her to do, for with looking forward to the day when all the things would come, the pleasure and excitement, there was times when she could hardly hold her horses. Tim had to sort of keep his eye on her, and sometimes when she seemed too tickled at the thought of the great time coming, or restless at the dragging of the days and she would come near giving things away to the whole family by her actions or maybe a word, that cowboy would let out a meaning cough or grunt and she'd always catch herself and quiet down at that and one of his looks. It was a tough spell of time for little Margie.

CHAPTER NINE

IT was also a tough spell of time for Tim. For just moseying around doing nothing but that and eating and sleeping wasn't his caliber, and the folks being all so doggone good to him made things all the worse and uncomfortable. He wanted to get out with Jake and Joshua and work with them at their wild horse trapping, and most of all he wanted to catch that Scorpion horse and be able to ride him again.

But mother nature takes her own good time about healing things and it wasn't until the first week in the month of December that Ophelia turned him loose as a healed man, with a severe warning that he should be careful for a while yet and that he shouldn't ride but very little and nothing but gentle stuff.

And by that time he had no chance to ride, for the folks was making ready to hit for the trading post and town and he'd have to take care of the ranch and do the chores and such.

The first week of December was a late time for Joshua to be taking his catch of wild horses to town and shipping point, but he wasn't losing by it, for there was more of the wild ones caught and to take in, and the one responsible for the delaying of the trip and shipping was none other than Tim himself.

He'd got Joshua out by himself a month or more before and told him of his plans for the coming Christmas. Joshua had bellered at first and would have none of Tim's spending his money that way. It would be fine and all that, he'd said, but he couldn't have him do it.

But Tim easy enough got his own way. All he had to do was to threaten to leave and then Ophelia wouldn't have the chance to go in town to do the Christmas shopping she'd set her heart to do that year. That would of been quite a landslide on Joshua's household and there'd been heck to pay.

"You don't mean that, do you?" Joshua had asked, scared and half peeved at Tim's renigging that way.

"You're doggone tooting I mean that," answers Tim, acting determined. "You do that for me or I'll hoof it out right now. I can't ride yet but I still can walk some."

So, after some discussing on the subject, Joshua had finally agreed, and when he seen how happy that made Tim, he'd also caught on the spirit. He also seen by then that Tim had only been bluffing and wouldn't of renigged nor spoiled Ophelia's plans for anything, and at that old Joshua thought again as much of Tim, which was going some.

So, that decided on and both working in cahoots as Tim had already done with little Margie there was some more plotting went on below the round corral. Of course there was only three left now that wasn't in on the secret, Ophelia, Jane, and Jake, but them three was sort of the main stem.

It had been figured then and to make things work

well that the trip was put off a month or more and until the first week in December. It would take a couple of weeks by the time the wild ones was taken on in and sold. It was planned that Joshua would wait until Ophelia and Jane had done their shopping and then, with the excuse that he'd have to wait a few days until the horses was sold, he'd send 'em on back. A day later Jake and him would get the stuff Tim had ordered, come on home with it and hide it all until Christmas day. In the time it would take to make the trip and the outfit all returned home it would make it just about right in time to prepare and fix things up for a *regular* Christmas.

The delaying of the trip until the first week in December had been fine with Ophelia, only she'd wanted to order a few things thru the mail order catalogs which she didn't want to get in town. So Jake had been told to saddle up and take her mail to the trading post, which went well with Tim, for he'd also wanted to send his mail in. That had been done plenty of time ahead, and all ordered would be sure to be at the town when Joshua and his family got there.

"One thing you want to make sure of, Joshua," Tim had said, grinning, "and that's to take plenty of horses along that you can pack all this stuff on." He'd told him how many would be needed and that had made Joshua scratch his head some.

* * *

The day come for the outfit to start out. A team was

harnessed for "Ophelia's buckboard" which was cached thirty miles away. On one of the horses was packed two cases of town clothes for her and Jane. Ophelia then got on her old saddle horse. She would lead the team, and little Margie would go along with her on her own little horse. Them two would go ahead, for it'd be some time before the mustangs could be rounded up, turned and handled in the pasture before they could be trusted to take out, and then that would have to be done slow and easy and mighty doggone careful so they wouldn't "kettle" (scare) and start running. For if any got to start running they'd scatter like a bunch of quail and, as happens in such cases, most likely all get away and back to the hills, when they'd be harder than ever to catch again. Taking 'em out of this pasture was ticklish work.

Tim figured he'd be fit to ride that day, and when Ophelia and her little daughter was started on their way he rode on to the pasture with Joshua, Jake, and Jane. The wild ones had been handled in the pasture for a couple of days, herd-breaking 'em, that is to have them so they'd turn as a rider would want 'em to, stay together and stop when they was wanted to. A wild horse is like an antelope and he has to be teached them things. That's herd-breaking 'em.

That had been done from the trap where they'd been caught, but after being in the pasture for quite a spell they had to be sort of herd broke over again. The two days that had been spent at doing that tamed 'em down a considerable, and so, there wasn't much trouble

She would lead the team, and little Margie would go along with her on her own little horse

getting 'em and holding 'em together that early morning and getting 'em lined out for the long trip ahead. But it was still mighty ticklish work, and Tim's help was more than welcome.

Joshua more than marvelled at the way he could handle wild horses, quiet and quick and at exactly the right place at the right time without a false move to spook 'em, and even as old a hand as Joshua was at the game he learned some more from Tim that morning, so did Jake, and as for Jane, she got to thinking she didn't know anything about wild horses after watching him and seeing how easy, smooth, and quick he worked, without any flash or any unnecessary moves. He was a mustanger.

There was not a slip nor the start of a run as the mustangs was eased out of the double gate of the pasture. It of course helped some that there was ten head of gentle horses mixed in with the wild ones, they was the horses that'd be used to pack on the way back, mostly saddle horses.

Tim and Joshua took the lead on the wild ones, and Jane and Jake the flank. Nobody was needed behind and all went well, so well that along before noon Tim grinned at the remark that he'd better get back to the ranch and tend to his chores.

"Don't buy out the town," he says to Jane as he rode by her, "and don't let none of them city slickers get you," he laughed. "Nor you either," he added on to Jake. "So long and good luck." And he started back for the ranch.

The ranch was a mighty lonely looking place when he got back there, looked like somebody had died there and even the ghost was asleep. The milk cows and pigs and chickens acted queer to him and as tho they was lonesome too, and after he done the chores and dark come he felt like he was in a graveyard. He never thought a place could get so desolate so sudden, and when he warmed over a meal that evening, after no noon meal, he couldn't get much taste out of the grub, even if it was Ophelia and Jane who'd cooked it, plenty of it for him.

After washing and putting away the dishes he tried to read some but he didn't know what he was reading was about, much. He thought of writing to Pete, for sort of company like, and he did scribble a few lines on a tablet he found on a shelf in the kitchen, but what he said was too much from a lonesome man and of course he said too much, aplenty to connect him with the northern happening in case the letter was opened by some inquisitive party. He also said too much of his whereabouts and that wouldn't do. But he felt like he was talking to somebody anyway, and when he got thru and put the letter in the stove he was more satisfied.

Not being used to riding for so long is what helped him some, he was tired, his side and shoulder hurt him a little but a night's sleep would fix that, so he finally went outside and crawled into his bed there.

He was awake before daybreak the next morning but he just layed and thought, thought of many things which just brought on more thoughts. He wasn't thinking so much about the present because all was fine now, too fine for him to take advantage of, and after

A Joshua

Christmas time, as soon as he caught Scorpion he'd be hitting out. He didn't know where to, but it would be somewhere in that country and where he could hole up for the winter. That country of Joshuas was the only safe one for him, nobody ever showed up in it much, and during the two months he'd been in it only one prospector driving a team of burros and a rider leading a pack horse had come to stop by the ranch, then went on.

Maybe Joshua would know of a place where he could locate and make a bluff at trapping horses, but maybe he'd better not ask Joshua because that old mustanger might insist on him staying. It would be best if he just let on that he was wanting or had to go somewhere and out of the country. He could buy a pack horse from him and he figured it would be safe enough to go to the trading post and supply up, then he could go from there.

As far as the money he had buried to the north, he didn't know what he'd do with that as yet, and since meeting Jane he wished he hadn't touched it, but it was too late now, and he figured he'd only get stomped on if he was to try and clear himself by returning it. But he'd been mighty apt to've done that, only the thought of being implicated with the killing of the two agents stopped him. He didn't know how things had or would turn out. He'd put his foot into something and now he wasn't going to stick his nose into it. So he decided to keep the money and make use of it the way he seen fit, also to sort of carry him thru the mess he'd got into. For he wouldn't dare get out of this country now and show himself in any settlement or town in daylight, and he'd be mighty handicapped in making a downright honest living for a long time, if ever. Even after many years he'd still feel fidgety and be on the dodge. So he'd just hole up somewhere in the country for the winter and forget about the money for a while. He had more than plenty to do him for a long time in that country, even after the Christmas shopping he'd done. He'd only need a pack horse and outfit and grub and he'd still have a few hundred left from the thousand he'd took out of the box, also a couple of thousand of his own. In the spring he could do some more fast night riding north, get the money and ride back. There'd sure be nobody out looking for him by then. The hold up would be forgotten by all excepting officers, and as long as he didn't show himself in no town he figured he'd be safe.

But this country is where he wanted to make his hang out, and wether he'd be on the dodge or not it would still be the country of his choice. Parts of it, the sage flats, reminded him of his home in Idaho, and he was happy here amongst wild horses and where people was few. He'd get Pete to come down with him and they'd get to running the wild ones. Maybe he could find a little country with enough water and good enough range so he could *raise* good horses, or cattle, and maybe he'd find a little out of the way outfit already running that he could buy.

He was afraid of only one thing and that was that he'd be kind of lonesome. He'd made camps alone aplenty, for a long time at a stretch and had never been lonesome before, but somehow since coming to this ranch something had happened to him and he didn't think he could hole up any more like he used to. There'd have to be some action and company.

Many thoughts and some lonesomeness vanished as the rays of the rising sun hit the edge of the canyon and brightened up the ranch and the country around. He'd been up and had a fire built by then, and the coffee pot was simmering on the kitchen stove. A few black cups of that and he lost more loneliness, and he was whistling as he went on to do the chores. After that he went on to turn the water to irrigate the garden and little hay patch.

That was all new kind of work to him, and as he puttered around that way he was surprised that he liked it. "Sure a homey little place," he thought, as he'd smoke and look around the neat ranch and then watch the water from the big spring above make its way thru little ditches and onto the driest patches.

The days would of drug on mighty slow if it hadn't been for the taking care of the ranch in general and the doing of the chores. He took his time and spent a lot of it at all of that and with that he didn't feel lonesome much until evening come, then he'd busy himself cooking up a batch of something or other that'd do to warm over for the next day. He didn't have much heart at batching right then, it'd be for too short a time and besides he didn't want to stir up any more in the kitchen than he could help.

As day would come he thought of riding out and see if he could get a glimspe of Scorpion but he'd have to be on hand to do the chores and take care of things, and that wouldn't leave him much time. Besides he didn't know what range the horse run on nor where the traps was located, and if he did get to see him he couldn't of done anything, for he didn't have a horse fast enough to ever catch up with him so he could rope him. It takes a mighty good horse to catch up to a good horse.

So he'd no more than think on the subject when he'd drop it and go on about his chores and irrigating. Then one day and while thinking of the Christmas doings it came to him sudden, what about a tree? There ought to be a Christmas tree.

But there was no spruce in that country. The closest that would come to such a tree for that Christmas decorating purpose was jack pine or piñon. One of them would do and would sure be a lot better than nothing, if he could find a right pretty one, for after all it wouldn't be so much the kind of tree that would count, it would be what was on it and the cheer and spirit around it. Even an old dry juniper would look good if that's there.

He took an axe and went out afoot and along the edge of the canyon looking for one, one day. There was none close but he could see a likely looking patch some miles away, so the next day he took a horse and rode over to it. He found one there, a right pretty little jack pine. He found something else too a-gliding thru the tall brush below him, it was a bunch of wild turkeys. They wasn't hunted in that country much and he got pretty close to 'em, but not close enough so he'd want to take a chance at 'em with his .45. He'd want to hit 'em in the head or neck, for a .45 slug in the body would sure ruin 'em.

So he didn't spook 'em by any chance shot at 'em. He rode back to the ranch with the tree over his shoulder, and like he'd seen it done at home, he set it up on a stand that day. The next day he took Joshua's 30.30 (there was no shotgun on the ranch) and he got two fine wild turkeys—and the next day, late in the afternoon, here comes Ophelia, Jane, and little Margie riding in.

The day after that, Tim rode out and met a pack train led by Joshua and brought up by Jake. It didn't get to the ranch until away after dark that night and the pack train was eased around into the corral as tho it was a gun running outfit.

The eve of the big day come, and being that little Margie was the only little one in the outfit, she was of course allowed to stay up with the big ones and enjoy the goings on, even to seeing the packages of presents her mother had got her. There was a lively twinkle in her eye as she looked at them and then at Tim, for she knew about what they was, and she knew what else she had coming.

A great fuss was made over the tree Tim had set up, and in the big kitchen, being decorated up as it was with little and big packages it got to look real Christmassy, even if there was no lights nor tinsel ornaments on it.

That all done and the women folks being tired from

He rode back to the ranch with the tree over his shoulder

the day's cooking and fixing, Joshua told 'em to hit for bed and take on a good rest because it was late and the next day would be a big day. Him and Tim and Jake would stay up for a spell yet and finish up.

"But there's nothing to finish up," says his wife, not at all suspicioning.

"Well," says Joshua, "I just thought we'd have another little shot of brandy. We don't get to celebrate often you know—you can stay up and have one with us if you want, you and Jane."

But they didn't want to stay up for that, and being tired as they was they went to their rooms, little Margie along with 'em.

"Don't mind us if we make a little noise," says Joshua to 'em as they went. "We might get a little loud but we'll try to be as quiet as we can."

"We won't even hear you," says Jane, smiling a "good night."

After waiting a while the three went out in the dark and brought in everything from the thick brush where it had all been hid a couple of nights before, all had been uncrated what needed uncrating. There was grunts of heavy lifting on some of the things but none was heard inside the house, the three worked as quiet as they possibly could. When all was brought in and the things stacked around the little tree it looked like a warehouse, and the tree, even tho it reached to the ceiling, was having a hard stand making a show of itself. Some of the biggest things had been set apart from it.

When everything had been brought in, Tim then told Joshua and Jake to hit for their soogans too, that he'd now take a little shot of brandy all by himself and this was his job from now on, the marking of the packages. It was an hour later when Tim finally went to his bed, a little tired but very happy, and a little scared of who all might fall on his neck on the next day.

And to make things seem more right a little flurry of snow fell that night. It was daybreak when Tim kicked it off his tarp the next morning. There'd been a runkus going on inside the house for near an hour and he'd just been laying in his bed, taking it all in and laughing.

He wouldn't of got up when he did, but Joshua had come out to get him, acting madder than a squeezed hornet. And he had been squeezed aplenty, and kissed too, both by his wife and daughter and at about the same time. For as they got up and opened the doors of their bed rooms the first thing that struck their eye was an upstanding and shining piano. Tied to it was a card saying "To my darling daughter from her loving father."

In another part of the kitchen was a sewing machine, a mighty pretty one and looked like a cabinet, and tied to it was a card saying "To my darling wife from her loving husband." They was fancy printed cards too.

With the sight of them two first things it was a wonder old Joshua didn't get smothered, and finally getting his breath and seeing the cause he come near blurting out who the real guilty party was. It was sure a wonder he didn't, and that's how come Tim was called in a rough way that morning. He figured they'd be falling on his neck, and at Joshua's call he sat up a-grinning and ready to take things as they came.

Tim slipped on his boots and pants as Joshua raved. "It ain't right, Jerry, and you know it. Them things ain't from me, they're from you, and I'm going to tell 'em."

"I know it's a dirty trick on you in a way," grins Tim when Joshua got thru. "But I had my reasons. For instance, it wouldn't look right for me to give your daughter such presents, then again she might think wrong of it, that maybe I'm trying to make a hit with her that way. With you giving her the piano that way you'd better give your wife something to sort of even things up, and that's where the sewing machine comes in."

"Yes," says Joshua, toning down some. "I've been wanting to get her one for years, and she's sure happy now."

"That's fine," says Tim, "and here's something else. You've sure earned them presents bringing 'em over here."

Joshua grinned. "It wasn't so bad," he says. "I had 'em hauled as far as I could and then strung two poles on two pack horses, one behind the other, and tied the piano up between 'em. I done the same thing with the sewing machine."

"Well, anyhow, and if it'll make you feel any better, them presents are from me to you for all you folks have done for me, and you just turned 'em over to your wife and daughter, that's all. It's mighty small returns, I think, but they're *your* presents to them. And a Merry Christmas to you, old timer," says Tim, as he stood up and stuck out his hand.

"The same to you, and many of 'em," says Joshua, now all happy. "But them presents are soon going to be found out because I'm going to tell 'em. Not today maybe but sure enough tomorrow."

Tim didn't say anything as to that for the time. He washed in the outside basin, combed his hair by the glass above it, and putting on his coat, he followed Joshua on into the house.

The two could hardly get in for the mixture of opened boxes, paper and all scattered as tho the house had been ransacked by a bunch of warring Indians. There was cheers and greetings of "Merry Christmas" as Tim walked in and the spirit was sure there. Jane was at her piano, with dresses and things spread all over it. Ophelia had done the same by her sewing machine.

Little Margie was packing dolls and toys from here to there, and Jake was admiring a flower stamped, well rigged and made saddle, there was also a colorful Navajo saddle blanket. He didn't know what to say to Tim about it, neither did the rest of the family for the presents he'd got 'em. But if any man ever got grateful and appreciative looks it was him that Christmas morning.

Jane reached over for a package, and handing it to

Joshua, she says, "Here's something for you from Jerry, Dad."

Joshua looked at Tim with another sort of peeved look and went to unwrapping the package. Then at the sight of what he dug out of the wrapping that peeved look just had to die. First there was a pearl handle .45 six shooter, right balance, length of barrel and all. He knew they cost $50.00, for he'd priced 'em once. Then there was a well made border stamp cartridge belt and holster, and that was just right too.

Joshua looked at Tim again, and there was near a sign of tears in his eyes as he says, "Doggone your hide, Jerry."

It seemed like the happiest time of his life for Tim, but he felt sort of uncomfortable at everybody being so grateful and wanting to say or do something in return. But a break come his way and gave him a chance to make a fuss too. Ophelia handed him a package, saying it was for him, then Jane handed him one. In Ophelia's package was a good and heavy mackinaw coat, something he sure needed, and in Jane's was two wool shirts and a black silk neckerchief. That sure came in fine too, for Tim'd had no chance to buy any clothes, and the only two shirts he'd had, wearing one on top of the other and relaying on 'em as he'd wash one and the other later, was pretty well frazzled out. One had been badly tore up by Scorpion and the other was wore thru at the elbows. Ophelia had mended 'em but they was near past that stage, and being the winter had come and it was now more than chilly the two heavy shirts sure came in good time, so did the neckerchief.

It was now Tim's turn not to be able to say anything. But there, Joshua came to his help by saying, "Let's have a couple of cups of coffee and a sip of brandy, Jerry."

At that, Ophelia throwed up her hands and broke away from all that was stacked on and around the sewing machine. "My land," she says, "we must have some breakfast," and Jane also broke away to help her.

"Never mind about any fussing around with breakfast," Joshua says to 'em. "Not this morning, not unless you're hungry yourselves. We haven't got time to eat, and besides if anybody is hungry there's plenty of fruit, nuts and candy and we can fill up on that. Looks to me like the whole outfit is already filled up that way now, and just this coffee to wash things down with is plenty fine for this morning, Ophelia."

Her and Jane kind of hesitated. Breakfast had always been the very first thing, but they was glad to forget it that morning. They both looked at one another, smiled happily and went back to what all they'd scattered about. There'd been no chirp about breakfast from Jake nor little Margie either, for they was both plum full and had no time for it.

"We'll eat at noon or any time we're good and ready," says Joshua.

That went well, and now that everybody had their presents and was busy over 'em they all felt at ease and to enjoying 'em to the limit. Tim thought he'd never enjoyed a sight more, and sometimes watching Jane's

There, feeding on a mangerful of hay, was a chestnut horse. It was Scorpion

expressions over this and that was worth many times what he'd got for her, or the whole family. It seemed more like home than even the good home which he'd had.

"Come on, Jerry," says Joshua, after he'd tried on his cartridge belt and then hung it up by his rifle. "Let's go outside for a spell. I want to show you something."

He led the way on down to the corral, and Tim followed, wondering. But he didn't have to wonder long, for coming around the corner of the horse shed in the square corral, Joshua stepped to one side and waved a hand to one end of the shed.

There, feeding on a mangerful of hay, was a chestnut horse. It was Scorpion.

CHAPTER TEN

CHRISTMAS wasn't over when that day was past. The spirit of that day would linger on until another Christmas come, and for years. For with the presents to all hands they'd be steady enjoyments and reminders of that day. Ophelia would never stop enjoying her sewing machine and making things on it. Jane would enjoy it too, along with her piano. With it was a whole printed course of piano lessons and she had a good ear to go along with that. Then there was a portable phonograph for a change of music, and a couple of dozen records to furnish it, which would break in or help with Jane's practising. That was enjoyed by the whole family.

Joshua's pearl handle six shooter would of course last many a life time, and it would never be lost nor "taken away from him." He babied it more than if it'd been a bejeweled crown with a thousand years of ancestry attached to it. As for Jake, his saddle and Navajo blanket would be under him and his admiration and love for many years to come. He'd tuck it away in good shelter and out of the weather and sun when work was done.

Little Margie would be the first one to run out. She wasn't at all destructive, but accidents sometimes happen to dolls. There wasn't much room for all her stuff along with Jane's in their bed room, and she might forget and leave 'em outside some night and then a rain come. But she was mighty careful and loving with her "family" and they would most likely last her until she near outgrowed 'em.

With the mackinaw and wool shirts which would last Tim thru the winter he had a plenty to cover his hide and keep it warm, and now, with Scorpion again, he was free to ramble on as he pleased and when he pleased.

But now that he could he wasn't at all anxious about it, and for two mighty good reasons. One was that none of the family would hear about it, and when he mentioned it one evening, after New Year's Day, little Margie looked at him, edged off into her bed room and went to crying. The rest of the outfit wasn't much better, and Ophelia's and Jane's eyes come pretty moist.

Joshua wouldn't trust himself to say anything, and Jake was the same. Both looked at the floor, and as Tim sized up the outfit he had to look away. It would be mighty hard to leave an outfit like that, more so when he had no special place to go only to hole up and by his lonesome.

So, seeing how he'd shaded the family's happy feelings by the mentioning of his going he managed to stir a cheerful smile as he turned to look at 'em, and he says, "Of course I don't know just when I'll be going as yet."

At that the family broke loose, relieved, and smiles

begin to reappear. Little Margie come out of the bed room, red eyes a shining. She'd heard him.

Then Ophelia sort of got after her husband for bringing "that horse" in. "You know very well that he's in no shape to ride such a horse for a long time and that he would try to ride him if you brought him in."

"Yes," Joshua agreed, sorry like, "I should of known."

Tim laughed, hearty now. "Why, that horse is all right," he says, "only you got to keep a-watching him."

But that horse wasn't all right. He'd been a regular wolf when Tim caught him in the afternoon of Christmas Day. Him and Joshua had been hitting the brandy pretty strong, and Joshua, again feeling that he could ride the rough ones, started for the corrals to prove that he could. But Ophelia and Jane had been on hand to see that he'd stomp no broncs that day nor any other day, and it went the same for Tim for the time being. He had to turn Scorpion loose again without even putting his saddle on him. Jake had been the only one allowed to ride. He had to try his new saddle, and he done that well on a young stud that'd been kept out of the wild bunch and which he was to break for a saddle horse.

So that afternoon had been passed without any events with Scorpion. But a couple of days later Tim had caught him again, and rode him. It had been wild goings on, and the chestnut brought on all his tricks, which made it good, for Tim, for then he sure *had* to

But there was no taking the buck out of such a horse

watch him. Scorpion was again as wild and wilder than when Pete had first caught him, only he was now all the wiser, and Tim had to use all of his skill in handling him.

With the dust being stirred in the corral the whole family had come down to watch the proceedings, Ophelia had been in the lead and with the intentions of stopping them proceedings, but it had been too late, for Tim had already been up and a-riding. It was then that the whole family realized he might ride away any day, and when he mentioned it they knew he could.

But from that ride Tim had felt he couldn't, his side had made that plain and his right shoulder and arm had been weak and not at all up to snuff. He'd tried to hide that, but Ophelia's wise eyes had noticed it, brought on some liniment and come near tying him down with bandages again.

He'd rode Scorpion again the next day and with the intentions of taking the buck out of that pony. But there was no taking the buck out of such a horse, he'd always buck and fight wherever and whenever he'd want to, and he couldn't be made to do either if he didn't want to. Tim soon found that out. It had been the first time he'd ever undertook to fight it out with him, he hadn't wanted to do it before because during the long ride from the north he'd been wanting to save all the strength and action that horse had for the single purpose of eating up distance with and not to waste a lot of it in one spot.

So, on that account he'd never fought it out with

him. But at the ranch now and *at home* there'd been a good time to find him out, and he did. He found out for sure that Scorpion would always be Scorpion.

He rode him most every day after that, outside the corral and sometimes along with Joshua and Jake as they'd go to patch up their traps or the cedar fence that made up the wild horse pasture to the edge of the canyon. The canyon rim went to make one side of it. Scorpion seemed to take to that and soon gentled. Tim couldn't of stood no long rides, and it was along while mending the cedar fence the day after he'd remarked he'd be leaving that Joshua took him to hand and begin to try and talk him out of it.

"Why, you know daggone well you ain't in no shape to ride, Jerry," he says once, while stopping to roll a smoke. "And supposing you get sick along the way to wherever you're going. . . . Where in samhill is it that's so all fired important that you got to go, anyway?" he asks.

"No place in particular," says Tim. That wasn't what he'd planned on saying but it had come out frank and before he could think. Then, being he'd stumbled this much, he figured he'd just as well go on with another thing he'd had on his mind. "I want to hunt me up a place," he went on, "a place something like yours and where I wouldn't be running in your territory."

"What's the matter with my place and my territory?"

Tim's grin was kind of serious. "It's fine, Joshua, all too fine for me to take advantage of, and besides

Jake is too young and wild himself to be real good help to me

you know I can't stay with you always. I've got to have a place of my own."

"Yeh, that's right," Joshua agrees. "A feller's got to have a place of his own." He looked at the ground, thinking hard, then after a spell he looked at Tim again and went on.

"But there's no special hurry about getting such a place, is there? Why don't you wait till you get real well, till spring anyhow, and if you feel like it in the meantime you can trap with me, then later on when the water holes dry up you can help me with the wild ones. Jake is too young and wild himself to be real good help to me. All he wants to do is run and ride 'em and he don't use much judgement when it comes to catching 'em. But with you I know there'd be twice the catch. There's lots of wild ones here and there's nobody bothering to catch them in this territory because I've took up the best places and built my traps on 'em. I'll give you a third of what's caught, and that's giving you the worst of the deal.

"Of course, it's out of the question to catch any at water traps this time a year on account of the rains and snows we've had and still going to have and water being most everywhere. Roping 'em would be too slow and too hard on our saddle stock, you know that. But we could build a blind trap or two. I know of some natural places where it wouldn't take us so long to build 'em and there's no doubt but what we could trap many mustangs mighty quick. Then I have plenty of cayote traps I could spare and you could attend a trap line that way in between times. There's the lions too, and we could work on all of that on shares, you getting a third and staying with us. I wish you would agree to work with me that way and stay."

If Joshua had of been a bachelor, Tim would of took him up on that in a second, but with his good family he felt he had no right to edge into it and share such a home. Then again he was afraid of what it might do to him to be where he'd be near and seeing Jane every day and then have to leave. He stared into space for a while, and thinking of how the folks had felt about his leaving and knowing he would *have* to leave, he says:

"Thanks very much for the proposition, Joshua. You folks are mighty good to me, and I'll think it over."

"Good," says Joshua; "you'll stay. And," he went on, "as far as a place is concerned, I know where there's one, a durn good one too, better and bigger than mine. It's on this same canyon, some forty miles from here, and setting just about like mine only there's more water there, a good sized meadow and big trees on it and around the house. Sure a pretty place, and closer to town than what I am. You can drive to it with a wagon from there when you need to, which is a big advantage. The old feller that owns it runs a little bunch of cattle there and a couple of stud bunches of horses too. Good range, no feeding necessary no time and good running springs."

Tim more than perked up his ears at that. "And that old feller would sell it?" he asks.

"Yes, he told me he wanted to." He's getting too old to run the place and he wants to go live in town with his married daughter the last few years he thinks he's got left. I figure a feller could get that place, stock and all, for $5,000 and I think it's sure worth it. Of course he's only got about 60 head of cows, but a man could run 500 head in that country as easy as not because there's no mustangs there to eat up the range, and that's the only drawback there is with that country, no mustangs."

Tim grinned. "I could come over here and get some."

"Them two stud bunches of his, about fifty head all together, are worth four times that many mustangs," says Joshua to that, "and they bring him near as much as his cattle do, and——"

Joshua checked himself right there. For he was making the place sound mighty good, too good, and even tho it was all true the glint he caught in Tim's eyes as he'd described the place put the fear in him that that cowboy might fly the coop any minute and hit for that paradise on earth. Just the place Tim had wanted.

It would be all right if there was no mustangs in that country, Tim was thinking. He would raise some valuable horses, and cattle too, and hole up more contented that way. But now as he thought of "holing up" he got to wondering.

"How's that country for people?" he asks. "Many of 'em there? I mean neighboring outfits or people travelling thru."

Joshua gave him a quick squint. "About the same as here," he says. "The closest neighbor is some twenty miles down country, only there's a main road about ten miles from the ranch that's travelled quite a bit and a few people drop up there once in a while."

Tim kind of grinned. "Not much of a place for a horsethief to hide out in then," he says.

Joshua's sudden suspicions came to the top. "Now what in samhill you been up to?" he asks.

Tim had planned to tell Joshua but not until he knew if he'd see any more of him or not and how close to him he'd be holing up. He had no mind of telling him now, only the place that'd just been described to him had got under his hide and he wanted to find out if he could well enough hide there. Joshua could tell him, or of some other place. And as far as the happening to the north was concerned, Tim now had no fear but that the telling of it to Joshua wouldn't be as safe with him as if he'd be telling it to a granite boulder.

So, in as few words as possible he told him the story of the happening. Joshua's expression hardly changed as he took it all in, and when Tim got thru he only remarked:

"Well, I don't know but what I'd done the same thing. But," he went on, "with the killing it sure does put you in a tough fix." He looked up at him. "Why in samhill didn't you tell me this before? I could of been on the lookout for you as I was riding and anybody come."

Tim told him the reason why he didn't tell him, that he didn't think he'd be staying in this perticular country long, and then Joshua came back at him that he'd *better stay* in this perticular country long and right at his home.

"There's no better place for you than my place," he says. "I can keep a-looking out for you, and with you not being in shape as yet is a double reason why you'd better decide to make camp with us and stay."

Tim shook his head, and now that he'd told the old mustanger so much there was only one thing more which he might just as well tell him and clear his chest of.

"I have no right to take advantage of you folks' hospitality and home when I'm *wanted* this way," he says, "and I wouldn't of done it only that I wasn't able to go on."

Then, wanting to have it all out, he went on to tell him of his caring for Jane, and of what might happen if he stayed. Another good reason why he shouldn't stay.

Joshua, surprised, pondered on that subject for quite a spell. His daughter Jane, that was a touchy proposition. He'd wanted the very best for her, and more too. He'd never thought of Tim for her, and now that he did he couldn't think of any one he would want more. But what all was hanging over that cowboy's head sort of put the kibosh on things. It wasn't that, according to the eyes of the law, he'd committed a crime, it was that he'd be hunted and maybe caught for it, and no home should be made and can be happy while that was threatening.

There's outlaws and outlaws, thought Joshua. He'd seen quite a few and of different kinds, for this desolate country of his was an open short cut to the border and safe for them to drift thru. Tim was outlawed, he figured, but he was no outlaw. He'd got to know and see thru him, and he'd trust him with what he cherished most in the world besides his wife. That was his daughter, Jane.

But considering all and how things was he decided it would be best if Tim went, and if there come a time when he cleared and exhonorated himself he'd be mighty, mighty glad to see him come back.

"How does Jane feel about it?" Joshua finally asks.

"About what?"

"About that happening to the north and your caring for her so."

"Why, I've never told her," says Tim, surprised that Joshua would even consider him in connection with her. "I don't know if she cares at all or not, and I've sure been hiding *my* feelings."

Joshua drawed a long breath of relief. He now had still more respect and affection for that reckless rider. He put his hand on his good shoulder.

"*White men* are few, son," he says. "Do as you think best. I'm with you and trusting you to the limit."

Then, like to help and give him freedom in his doings, he told him of another place and where he could sure enough hide out. It was along the canyon too, but up it and the opposite direction of the first place that

A trade rat, in a mighty desolate and dry country

had been described. This second place was only a wild horse camp. There was a dugout hid away from a spring, in a mighty desolate and dry country, the only spring for twenty miles around, and on that spring was a corral where, in the dry months, the mustangs of that country would come inside of to water. It was a water trap.

Few people knew of that place and on account of the country being mighty rough and no indication of water being in it, it was skirted around by most of the few riders going thru.

"It ain't no place like the first one I've described," says Joshua, "but you could sure feel safe there, where I sure wouldn't at the first place, not if I was in your boots, for there, being so close to a main travelled road a sheriff or anybody might drop in on you any time, not often maybe, but once is enough if the party happens to know about you.

"Now," he went on, "I'm sure doggone sorry that you feel you have to leave. You're sure welcome to stay as long as you want. You know how we all feel towards you, and it's going to be quite a blow to the whole family to see you go. So, I'd sure like to have you stay as long as you can."

There was no words that Tim could say to that, none that would begin to show his feelings of appreciation. He just held out his hand to Joshua who gripped it and he only said, "I'll stay as long as I can, old timer."

CHAPTER ELEVEN

THE staying wasn't at all easy for Tim, and even tho he hated the thought of hibernating by himself, leaving all that was here and where he'd been so happy, the leaving and hibernating wouldn't be as hard as the staying.

And now that he'd told her father he was all the more conscious of his feelings toward Jane. She seemed to sense that something had been stirred that way, making her all the more pretty in realizing and like agreeing. More and more now he caught her looking at him with a light in her eyes that scared him. He was scared as much for her as for himself as he thought of the hurt in the parting that was to come.

From the time he'd had the talk and understanding with Joshua he figured on staying at least another month, or maybe till spring, all depended on his feelings for Jane and if he could suffer along keeping 'em hid while seeing her every day. He hadn't accounted for hers, and now that they seemed to crop up and fast getting stronger for him, he was fast making up his mind to line out.

One evening settled it, and after only a week out of the month he'd planned on staying. He was down by the corrals that evening, all alone, leaning on the middle bars and stargazing thru the top ones when he heard footsteps coming up behind him. He recognized them footsteps and he turned to face Jane, her pretty face sort of flushed and lit up with a smile. What was back of that smile and what he seen in her eyes as he talked to her took all of his will power to talk at all without saying a word of what he wanted to talk about the most. It was cold there by the corral, but it was near dark when they turned to go to the house, and that night Tim had decided.

He'd decided to hit out before he lost a stirrup, and make it as sudden as he could. For if there was to be a blow, he figured it would be better to have it sudden than lingering.

So, before breakfast the next morning, he caught up Scorpion and got him saddled and ready, his few belongings he tied on behind the cantle. He would, as he'd planned, ride to the trading post, outfit there and hit out for a hiding place, the wild horse camp which Joshua had told him of. He would also get a pack horse at the trading post, saving him the trouble of leading one there, and the dickering for one from Joshua, for Joshua wouldn't of dickered, he'd just wanted to *give* him one. Tim was sure of that, and he couldn't of accepted.

He wouldn't have to hide out long, he figured, just a couple of months or so and then he would hit north and dig up the money he'd cached there. He didn't know what he'd do with the money, excepting to cache it again where he could get at it easier whenever he'd need some. As far as to where he'd go then, he'd talk that over with Pete, and maybe with him hit for some other far away range where people was few. With all such goings on and time he'd be sort of healed from the hurt his riding away from Jane would give him, and he would never want to come back to any part of this country again and be reminded of her that way, not unless he was cleared of what was hanging over him, and that he couldn't hope for.

He'd thought that all out during the night, and it being decided on, he done his best to act as usual during the breakfast and when all gathered at the table on early morning.

He waited until breakfast was well over, and then, before the family scattered to chores and different works, he spoke up with a smile and told of his leaving, that his horse was saddled and he was going right now. He didn't want to see, and he let on he didn't see how surprised and hurt the whole family looked and acted.

He went to say how he appreciated the hospitality and all they'd done for him and how he would somehow like to repay 'em, but, more for Jane's ears, a sudden hurt and the sooner to make her forget, he said that he would never be back in this country again, lying that he had a friend in South America who was in the cow business and he figured on going down there to stay.

He looked mostly at Joshua or the stove as he spoke, and as he went to shaking hands all around his hand didn't linger none, a bit longer in Jane's little trembling hand, and as he smiled at her he felt that the armor he'd willed over his face was sure to crack. The last was little Margie, who had both hands over her face and was crying. There was no handshaking there, so Tim kissed her on the forehead, and patting her on the back, started for the door and with a final sounding "Good bye" went outside.

Joshua and Jake followed him on out and on down to the corral, but neither tried to hold him back, and Joshua only remarked that he'd sure made up his mind sudden.

But he also seen that it was for the best. He only watched Tim who was sort of like walking in his sleep as he went to untie Scorpion and got on him. Scorpion acted gentle that morning, as quiet as Ophelia's old horse, and started out at a good distance eating walk.

But a short ways from the corral he spooked, and looking for the cause, Tim seen Jane coming towards him. He stopped Scorpion then and got off of him. He wished she hadn't come, for it would make the parting and going on all the harder.

"I'm going to walk with you just a short distance," she says, smiling but not doing a very good job of it.

Tim smiled too and said he was glad, but his armor was gone and his smile wasn't much better than hers.

The two walked on a ways, Tim leading Scorpion, and neither him nor Jane saying a word. They walked on for quite a ways, and finally feeling that the strain on 'em should be sort of broke, Tim thought he could speak.

"I sure hate to leave you folks," he begins, "but I

should of been down there with that friend of mine in South America long ago, and I would have been too if I hadn't got hurt the way I did, and then had to impose on you."

"And I'd never got to meeting you," says Jane, looking straight ahead. Then stopping and facing him, she went on, "I don't believe you're going to a friend in South America. There's something else."

Tim wasn't much surprised at that. He took her hand, she looked at him thru moist eyes, and when he spoke his voice was like an echo. "There is something else, Jane," he says, "very much of something else," and then come the hardest part. "This is good bye, Jane. You'll be happier soon."

He didn't know how close to the truth he was with that last remark. Not trusting himself any further he turned to get on his horse his mind all in a whirl. He hardly knew where he was or realized what he was doing when he stuck his foot in the stirrup and begin raising himself in the saddle. He felt like a ton of lead. . . . And that's just how he hit the earth a second later, like a ton of lead. For Scorpion had unwound of a mighty sudden and lit into hard and wicked bucking before Tim could come out of his trance and before he'd got into the saddle. He was throwed high, plum over the saddle, to land on his head and bad shoulder on the other side, leaving him sprawled out on the ground and unconscious there.

What went on from there would of been mighty well worth seeing to Tim. For Jane, quick as lightning, had caught the long and dragging hackamore rope before Scorpion had quit bucking and got to running, and jerking him to a stop climbed into the saddle before he got to breathing. In another couple of seconds and in the fastest gait he'd ever been put to she rode him to the corrals where she more than surprised Joshua and Jake.

There was no time spent on explaining and wondering, and as Joshua and Jake had been saddling up it was only a few more minutes before they was by Tim's side. But he was up when they rode onto him this time, and outside of looking a little dazed he seemed all right, all excepting for that right shoulder of his. It slumped limp.

It was some time later when supporting himself with his good arm on Joshua's saddle horse he came to the house. Ophelia and little Margie came outside to meet the outfit, and Tim managed to grin at 'em kind of sheepish. "The same thing over again," he says to Ophelia.

To see him come back, little Margie let out a squeal of joy. She didn't care much how he got back as long as he did and he was still alive. Her "mom" could fix him up. As for Ophelia, she felt near the same way, so did the rest of the outfit, and instead of Tim seeing sad or concerned looks on their faces all he seen was smiles, and some sympathy.

"The same thing over again," as Tim had said, meant just that. His collar bone had been broken over, his shoulder had been near dislocated and the cracked

In the fastest gait he'd ever been put to she rode him to the corrals

shoulder blade had been cracked some more. His side hadn't been helped by the hard landing on the rocky ground either but that didn't tally up to other parts as to harm.

All doctored up and bandaged over again, Tim was all set for another spell of forced idleness. He didn't like the thought of that much, for being he'd made up his mind to go and it had been so hard to do he'd of liked to went on. It had been hard and painful doings and all of no use, spoiled in one second and the more he come to his senses the more he felt ashamed and disappointed at coming back, coming back in such a shape and letting the same horse get him down a second time.

But there was no getting out of it, only this time he wouldn't be idle as long as the first time, he figured. His side wasn't bothering him so much and he thought that in two or three weeks he would be able to ride away again, even if his right arm and shoulder would still have to be bandaged up. It would be a big handicap, specially on such a horse as Scorpion, but he was determined to go, go any place and away from this hurt of hiding his feelings from Jane and, as he felt, taking the hospitality of these good people without seeing any chance of doing anything in return.

The weather being cold and stormy, the cot had been brought inside and a bed made up for him in the kitchen. It was a big kitchen as big as a good sized living room which it also served the purpose of, and there was plenty of space for it there, but Tim balked at taking any space in it. He might use a chair in there during the day and if it was cold, he said, but he wanted to be out of the way and outside at night.

They finally gave in to him, but they wouldn't let him be plum outside and in the open, so Joshua and Jake set him up a tent, one they sometimes used at wild horse traps or on the long trips to town. There was a stove pipe hole in the roof and inside they set up a little tin stove which would throw plenty of heat whenever it was needed.

"Doggone 'em," thought Tim; "can't stop 'em."

All the trouble and care they went to only made him feel uncomfortable, and he cussed the luck for this second happening, and himself too for not watching.

There was no laying him down this time, he was too mad and he told Ophelia so, but grinning the while, and to please her he sort of stretched out in a big horse hide chair as she asked, and let her cover him up, warning him again about fevers coming on at such times.

And now, being his arm and hand was bandaged tight to his body as before, Jane again took the job of rolling cigarettes for him. She seemed mighty pleased at the chance, but her nearness at such times only made Tim's good arm ache, ache near as much as the hurt one in wanting to touch her. But he just suffered along, aching, and he made up his mind that in spite of all and everything he'd be well again soon and he'd be riding on.

He wished he could get away from the sight of Jane

more and that she wouldn't look at him so often. He couldn't help but keep his eyes on her and watch every move she made, for she was a mighty good sight for anything that might ail a man but it didn't do his heart any good, not when it was anchored down with a load that wouldn't release it. And when that afternoon he wanted to go to his tent with the excuse that he wanted to stretch out, Ophelia won and he was talked into staying where he was.

"You can stretch out all you want on that chair," she says, kind of firm. "It's bad enough that you'll sleep there at night without going in the day time. Besides," she went on, "it's starting to storm and getting colder."

That settled it, and Tim cussed the luck some more. It was starting to storm sure enough, the wind was blowing and big snow flakes was passing straight by like they never was going to land.

"It *does* look like we're going to have some weather all right," says Tim, trying his best to show some cheerfulness.

"Yes," says Ophelia, "and for two cents I'd have that bed brought right back in here. Why, you'll freeze your ears out there unless you keep 'em under cover."

Tim grinned as Jane looked at him and smiled. "Doggone her," he thought, "I wish she wouldn't smile so pretty that way."

He felt sort of relieved when Joshua and Jake rode in that evening and with the news that they'd got another lion. The pleased looks on their faces cheered him up some, and as they went to telling how and where they treed him, that all took Tim's eyes and mind away from Jane and the edge off the disappointment on his start at leaving.

The lion was a big one. "You must be bringing me luck, Jerry," Joshua says, grinning. "I've been after that lion for a long time and I just get him when you're back here today. Then again, me and Jake caught some mustangs last fall that we'd been trying to get for a couple of years, like that bunch Scorpion was running with for instance, we didn't get 'em till you come and we've layed for 'em time and time again, run 'em and done everything we could to catch 'em before that for more than two years, but no chance, not till you come. We caught more horses since you been here than we did all last summer, some of the hardest bunches too and which we'd just about given up trying to catch."

"Well, I'm sure glad for that," says Tim, pleased to hear. "But doggone it, the kind of luck I been a-having sure don't treat me that way," he grinned. "It must take it out on me for the good it does you."

"Yep, it does work that way sometimes," Joshua agreed, and not at all seeming sorry about it. "But I don't see where you got any beller a-coming, young feller. You've got a good place to *hole up* in." He winked at him at that, meaning that it was a heap better than where he'd planned on going. A secret with him and Tim. "It's nice and warm here, plenty of good grub, reading and company, and music too." He looked at his daughter and smiled, "And pretty soon you'll be all right again, along about springtime. A mighty good time.

"Yessir." He went on after a while: "I think old lady luck is pretty good to you at that. Supposing for instance it had happened out away from here and thirty miles from water."

"Yep, and I might of broke my neck too," Tim added on.

"That wouldn't been so bad as trying to find a water hole and care when you're near out of your head with suffering," answered Joshua, kind of joking. "But anyway, as I rode out of here this morning, before I got set on the lion, I got to thinking about that Scorpion horse of yours, and the more I got to thinking, about how he layed you out so close to here the first time and again as you started to leave, it strikes me like he's in cahoots with something, or something is handling him. I've never seen a horse act the way he does. Like with Jane, she got on him and rode him to come and get us right after he piled you, she rode him back with us to get you and back here again, then unsaddled him and turned him in the corral, and I swear he was as kind and gentle as Margie's little horse. I could hardly believe my eyes."

"That's when he's most apt to get you," says Tim.

"And I wouldn't try that again," Jane chips in. "If I hadn't been so excited I'd never thought of getting on him. . . . He acted gentle and kind when Jerry started out this morning too, and look what happened."

Old Joshua shook his head. "I know," he says, "but not in the same way he did with you, Jane. I was down by the corrals when Jerry got on him and rode away. The horse acted gentle and all that but I could feel something was up when I come near him, not very strong but strong enough so I remember it now. But when you was on him and I come near, I didn't have that feeling at all, it was like you'd been sitting on your own gentle horse. . . . I might be all wrong but I wouldn't be afraid to have you ride him any time, Jane, night or day and rain or shine." Then turning to Tim: "But I would be afraid for you to do that," he says, "that is if you was to try and do something that wasn't in the cards for you to do."

"Like going to South America, for instance," grins Tim, looking up at Jane. Then he asked, "But supposing Jane was riding him and started out to do something that wasn't in the cards for her to do. What then?"

"Well, as I've said before, he acts different with her than he does with you. He doesn't seem to care what *she* does, he give me that feeling, and I'm sure she could go any place on him and do as she pleases and he wouldn't make one bad move. That horse is cut out for you, Jerry, and you only, and even tho he might be ornery and treacherous with somebody else there wouldn't be no point to it. If anything happened it'd be just a plain accident as might happen anywhere, like with any ordinary bronc. But with you it's very different. He seems on this earth to shape things up for you."

"And cripple me up doing it," says Tim, sort of dry.

Supper was being cooked while all this went on. Lamps had been lit, the supper put on the table, and the discussion went on thru the meal.

"And what about that cowboy he crippled up before I got him?" asks Tim, as he sat on his chair with a plate on his lap. "Was he trying to handle his future for him too?"

The family laughed, all but Ophelia, and Joshua went on, serious. Pointing his knife at Tim, he says: "That's all the more proof that that horse was cut out for you. If the cowboy you speak of hadn't got crippled up in the way you once told me he did and by that same horse, he wouldn't of had that accident, and if he hadn't had that accident you'd never got that horse, because then he'd been turned in with other broncs and at work on round-up."

That was true enough, Tim thought. He nodded, agreeing.

"Now, here's another thing I'd just as well say while I'm on the subject," Joshua went on, between bites, "I'm not afraid for Jane to ride Scorpion, but I would be afraid for myself or Jake here. I'm thinking he'd be like a regular bronc with us and much worse than the average, he'd be as mean with us as he is with you only in a different way. Now don't laugh but he's took on Jane too, but only to be kind and do all he can for her, nothing else. That's part of what he's on this earth to do, I think, and if you don't believe me we'll all go down to the corral some nice day and I'll prove it to you. I'll show you that he'll be plum gentle with Jane and turn out to be a regular wolf with either me or Jake.

"I know because I've tried to touch him a few times. I tried to touch him this morning a minute after Jane turned him loose and he was altogether a different horse that quick. Just like he was when me and Jake caught him and first brought him to the corral here before Christmas. Now how do you account for that?"

He looked around, even at little Margie, and there was no answer nor remarks. He went on: "I tell you, this Scorpion horse is a heap more than just a horse, he's Providence and Destiny and he does as it's pointed out for him to do, and he might be Fate too if that time comes while he's still alive. I've never seen the likes in anything, let alone a horse."

All was solemn around the table, even Tim who hid a grin. Then Ophelia spoke up. "Josh knows horses," she says to Tim. "That's all he knows besides 'cats' (catamounts) and I believe he's right. It sure strikes me like it when you stop to think that he'd crippled a man so you'd get him, then packed you from wherever you came from all the way here without doing you any harm, how he dropped you here and dropped you again when you started to leave. Yes, Jerry, I think Josh is right."

Tim just had to break loose with his grin at that. "Maybe you're both right," he says. "But doggone it

But you'll never lose *that* horse

I wish he'd give me an inkling as to what he wants me to do without busting me all up to make me see."

"And that brings another thing to mind," Joshua chips in, not so serious now. "He might be Opportunity, too. You know how Opportunity knocks, and how sometimes it knocks and nobody hears or realizes? Well, if he's Opportunity he'll sure make you realize, you can bank on that."

"Yeh," says Tim, "if he leaves me something to realize with."

"If he don't," laughed Joshua, "why then he's Fate."

"Some horse I've got. Now I suppose that if he don't try to cripple me when I try to ride him out of here again that all will be all right, and if he does why I should stay."

"If he does I guess you'd *have* to stay," says Joshua. "But laying all joking aside, I believe that this horse is here and cut out to you for some certain purpose. I'd pay attention to that if I was you and for 'better or for worse,'" he winked, "I'd sort of take it easy, not fret or rush, and see what comes of it."

From acrost the table, Jane shot a quick glance at Tim and just at the right time to meet his quick glance.

"And with all the other good proofs of Destiny or Providence having plenty to do with that horse"—Joshua was going on, speaking to Tim—"here's one more. That's that you didn't lose him when he layed you down at the spring where he first found you. Nine horses out of ten, and specially his kind, would of hit plum out of the country and you'd never seen him again. But you'll never lose *that* horse, he'll always be around and in one way or another make himself needed and handy to you for as long as he lives. He might be rough at times but he'll show you the way."

CHAPTER TWELVE

A FIRE had been built in the tent that had been set up for Tim, and when the talk of the evening was over, the main subject being Scorpion, and he went to the tent, it was good and warm in there. Joshua went along to see that he would be well covered up, and then like for a "good night" he said, "Take it easy, Tim, and don't fret. Jane and all of us are of course very sorry of your being hurt, but that couldn't be helped, and as it is we're mighty happy that you're here again and to stay, for a while at least. That ought to make you happy too, and it wouldn't hurt if you was more sociable with Jane, like you are with the rest of us."

With that he went outside and tied the tent flap for the night. That meant "sleep well." But no sleep came to Tim for a long time. His shoulder and side was paining him, had pained him ever since the numbness left him that morning. If it hadn't been for that he might of took things more cheerful that day. But his hurts, his plans being snagged so sudden and then realizing his helplessness had all went to irritate him. He'd enjoyed the talk of the evening more if it hadn't been for the pains that was physical. They wasn't so bad, just mighty aggravating and sort of went with his mental pains. He'd sort of forgot his mental pains while the talk had been about Scorpion, and now as he tossed a little, listened to the cheerful crackling of the wood in the little stove while the tent flapped to the wind and snow, Scorpion came back to him.

It had been a mighty big surprise that Jane had rode the horse to get help that morning, and to hear how she got along so well with him meant a heap more to Tim than just that, especially at the time when Scorpion's ornery streak had just come to the top.

It was past him to figure that out. Scorpion was kind and gentle to Jane, a raw bronc with Joshua and Jake, and a sleeping volcano that busted loose at picked times with him.

But even at that Tim couldn't put much faith in what all had been said about that horse being a horse of Destiny, cut out to control his and such, it was all so spooky and unbelievable. Then again, thinking it over as he was now doing and from the time he first caught him till now it did seem like that horse *was* playing a big part that way. He didn't know how it would all wind up but, as Joshua had said, "Scorpion would show him the way. . . . Pay attention and take it easy."

But it would be sort of hard to take it easy there, with Jane around, and maybe he should take Joshua's advice and be more sociable with her. He appreciated his telling him that she was happy, now that he would have to stay for a spell. He'd noticed that and it had made him happy too, but it had hurt him at the same time and he'd of been more at ease if she didn't care.

As he tossed now and again he got to thinking of ways of how he could leave as soon as possible. He thought that maybe in another week he could ride again, he could ride as far as to where the buggy was cached, then he could have either Joshua or Jake take him on in to the Trading Post. He could most likely find some place to stay there and get taken care of. He could ride a gentle horse and leave Scorpion behind, to his own Destiny.

He finally went to sleep thinking of Jane, Scorpion and his queer ways, and his plans of leaving. The crackling sounds from the little stove died away and it gradually turned cold in the tent, but Tim was well covered up and he slept well.

When morning come the ground was white with a good blanket of snow. Good for lion or deer hunting, thought Joshua, as he came out of the house and went to untying the flap of Tim's tent.

"You know," he says, as a good morning, "I dreamed about Scorpion last night. He was at the end of a rainbow, packing a sack of gold and grazing on the prettiest flowers I ever seen."

"Must of been pretty," grins Tim as he sat up. It was cold in the tent, but washing from the basin of water Joshua had brought him and then dressing, it wasn't long when he was ready to hit for the warmth of the house.

He sat at the table that morning, and with a few cups of coffee and surrounded by all the cheerful faces he had to be cheerful too, and even if his hurts had bothered him he'd of smiled along with the rest, but his hurts wasn't bothering him much that morning. The main hurt was that he had to be still.

There was some talk about Scorpion again during the breakfast, but not for long. The fresh snow had brought on other interest for the time and that was to track down some venison. A mighty good day, for the storm was over and it now was clear and still.

Right after breakfast, Tim was left to the ladies, and Joshua and Jake each taking a rifle (Joshua proudly belting on his pearl handled .45) went out and on down to the corral to saddle up. They didn't take the hounds they used for lion hunting that morning.

Having decided on a country to hit for to get their meat the two rode along side by side and as usual talking about mustang traps, cayote traps, lion hunting and all such. But that morning the talk also took on Scorpion, his queer way of acting, and the happening of the morning before, and the more the two talked on the subject the more spooky and mysterious it got to 'em, finally both coming to conclude that there sure was something super back of that horse's actions and which wasn't of his own accord.

The two talked on till they got to the hunting ground, then they begin watching for signs. They crossed antelope tracks which came from the flats and headed for the canyon for shelter during the last storm. They didn't want no antelope, for not much more than the hind quarters was any good on them and they could get antelope most any time. There was quite a bit

When morning come the ground was white with a good blanket of snow

more meat in a deer, not so dry and better tasting, and that's what they was after. Deer was harder to get than antelope, and with this fresh snow now was the time.

The two got all the quieter and more careful as they came to little jack pine forests, clearings and breaks. The deer country.

Keeping clear of dry limbs that would snap and make a noise, also from brushing against trees all they could, they rode on deeper in that country, their horses' hoofs hardly making a sound in the soft snow. The still air was also to their advantage, and even tho they hadn't as yet come to a single deer track, there was no telling but what they might come to a bunch browsing or hid away, still and just sunning themselves. So they acted according, kept watchful and was prepared.

And it was well they was prepared, for Joshua's sharp eyes barely got to squint over a rise, and only them and his light hat was showing when he made a motion to Jake, squatted low on his horse and then got off of him, tying him to a tree close by. Jake done the same, then the two taking their hats off and carrying 'em with their ready rifles eased on, on foot to where they could see their game.

When spotting game that way, neither Joshua nor Jake usually went to the trouble of tying up their horses and going on afoot the way they was now doing. They would only get off their horses for a better aim but they would keep the bridle rein in the crook of the arm or under a foot as they aimed.

But this time was not ordinary. Joshua had seen a lone buck, a big one and with many points on his wide antler spread, but the size and sight of the lone buck wasn't what had made him more precautious this perticular time, it was the way he acted.

Rifles ready for quick action, Joshua and Jake eased their way up to where they could see thru some brush. Only about three hundred yards away was the big lone buck, still standing where Joshua had first seen him but mighty alert for some reason, and that's why Joshua had been so precautious, to find out the reason.

He knew the buck hadn't scented nor heard him nor Jake or the horses, it was something else, closer, and the buck was trying to locate where the scent came from before he leaped away from whatever the danger was. He didn't want to leap into that danger and the scent of it seemed hard for him to locate in the still air.

So, while he stood all tense, head and ears up and alert, Joshua's and Jake's eyes went over every rock and clump of brush or trees around the buck, then finally, on the top of a ledge, and tipping some brush that'd took root there, Joshua's experienced eyes caught sight of a strip of yellowish hide. "Lion" came to his mind as quick as he seen it. He'd suspicioned it would be.

A whisper or two to Jake and they both levelled their rifles.

The lion was crouched low, tense as the buck below him and just waiting until his intended victim came

The lion was crouchea low, tense as the buck below him

closer, for as it was now there was too much distance by some feet for him to risk a leap.

They sighted. Three hundred yards would be an easy shot. The timing for shooting came with Joshua's nod and then, sounding like one, both rifles spoke, the buck slumped into the snow, and the mountain lion, screaming, lunged many feet into the air, missing the ledge coming down. When he landed, not far from the buck, he was also dead.

Joshua and Jake stood up and slowly started for their game and prey, ready to shoot again if they showed sign of life. But neither had hardly moved after the shots, and when the two hunters came near, still hardly believing their double good luck, they was surprised some more at the size of the animals. The lion was as big as the biggest Joshua had ever seen, and he'd seen many. As for the buck he ranked the same in his estimation.

Scratching his head in wonder and admiration, he says to Jake: "I don't know as I've ever even heard tell of such doings, not even by the biggest liars at the town bar. I'd be apt to doubt it myself if I wasn't sure I'm right here. I'll make more sure by skinning the lion right now. You bleed and gut the buck, Jake."

With more remarks as to the size of the animals and the double good luck of getting 'em, they both went to work and soon enough had the job done. The buck was strung up high on a stout limb. It would need a pack horse for that heavy a carcass, and either Joshua or Jake would come and get it on the next day. But the lion hide Joshua throwed in front of his saddle. That wasn't so heavy so it couldn't be taken right on in, even if it was a mighty big hide.

"That was a good shot you made, son," says Joshua to Jake as the two started back for the ranch. "Right thru the shoulder blade and straight to the heart."

Jake grinned, pleased. "You didn't do so bad yourself, Pap, considering how little you could see of that lion. He was broadside to you and you got him back of the shoulder and straight center to the heart too."

"Yeh, I couldn't see his head behind the brush. But I guess neither even heard the reports of our rifles, they was dead that quick."

It was a proud and happy pair of hunters that rode into the ranch. It was early afternoon when they got there, and being it was so early, Jake hurried thru a few bites, changed horses, and taking a pack horse went to get the carcass of the deer, leaving Joshua to tell of the good hunting that had been done.

"Yessir, Jerry," the pleased Joshua grinned. "You sure bring me good luck. Ophelia done me fine that way, meaning my family and home and real happiness." His wife looked at him, appreciating. "But your luck comes in from outside, with my trapping and hunting. I've never had such luck before that way. I've rode and trapped and hunted in this country for forty years and seen and heard of all kinds of happenings but not until today did I ever see or hear of a lion ready and waiting to pounce on a deer, and then have the good luck of getting them both."

"That's a scarce sight to behold all right," agrees Tim. "But as far as the good luck comes in I think Scorpion is responsible for that, the horse of Destiny, you know."

That day had been more pleasant for Tim. His hurts didn't bother him as much as the day before. The sun a-shining had helped brighten his spirits and took the edge off his disappointment. He then come to decide to follow Joshua's advice, of taking it easy and not fret, also to be more sociable to Jane, which was mighty easy for him to do and eased his feelings a considerable. She played on her piano for a few minutes once in a while, Tim hardly knowing if her playing was good or bad, nor caring. Watching her was plenty good. Then he would read a little or play the phonograph, and with the talking in between, Jane sitting by him and rolling cigarettes for him every now and again, he got to thinking he could stand it all well enough. He would "take it easy and wait and see what come of it." In the meantime he'd be sociable as he dared with Jane, but he wouldn't get ahead of himself so that when another time come for them to part neither would feel so hurt.

That worked all right for a while, and Tim's will power held fair enough. But as day after day passed and Jane got to seem even sweeter he feared of what he figured was sure to come, if he stayed much longer. Something would have to be done.

In the tent one evening he started to talk Joshua into taking him to the Trading Post, as he'd planned, but he didn't get far at that and it didn't take Joshua long to convince him that there was sure no place for him. Worse than any big town, he said, because with the few people at the Post he'd be noticed, wondered and talked about first thing. As they read the papers and some do nothing but loaf around and watch for easy money, and the happening to the north being still sort of fresh, some of them loafers, and even busy folks would be bound to remember.

"They might even have a description of you at the general store where the post office is," says Joshua, "and notice of reward. Then there's a constable there too who has nothing much to do and sure sizes up the few strangers that comes. Another thing, there's travellers come thru there in automobiles and horseback, and from long distances. Some of them might have your description in their tally books, you know, and hoping to run acrost you sometime. Five thousand dollars is mighty well worth picking up and watching out for. Some of them tin horn gazabos there would sell their grandmother's false teeth or give her away for ten dollars.

"No, Jerry, that's no place for you. It might be all right just to go in and supply up and get right out again. But to stay any length of time you'd sure be taking chances. If you had to go you'd ought to hit for a big town, the bigger the better and where there's lots of people, trade your boots off for spats and slippers, your hat for a cap, and with a suit of clothes you might pass in a crowd without being noticed. But I'd sure feel spooky myself and get cross-eyes watching everybody, for fear one out of the crowds would be tapping me on the shoulder any minute and ordering me to come along.

"What's wrong?" he went on to ask Tim. "And why so anxious to leave all of a sudden again? Are your affections for Jane getting the best of you?"

"Yes," says Tim. "And I'm wanting to leave for her sake too as well as mine."

"Why? Is she afflicted too?" Joshua had to grin.

"Yes. I'm afraid so. To tell the truth, I know so."

"Well . . ." Joshua, serious now, thought on the subject for a spell. When he spoke it was like sort of final. "If that's the case, and to keep from hurting one another I'm advising you to stay and make the best of it. If you and Jane are willing to take the chance, Ophelia and me will."

Tim looked at Joshua, surprised and mighty grateful, but not willing. "Why, you wouldn't want me as a son-in-law while I'm wanted and apt to be caught any time, would you?"

"You speak to Jane about that, Jerry. With me it goes as I've already said. Of course," he went on, "you don't have to rush things. Bear along as long as you can. In another year or so the mix up you got into will be forgotten by all but the officers of the railroad. But they sure don't know which way you went and you're safe here. Yes, and by then you'd even be safe at Old Walters' place, the pretty place down the canyon which I told you about once. In the meantime we maybe can dig up something that would clear you, or something might happen that will.

"So, as I've said before, take it easy and don't fret, neither you nor Jane, and make up your mind to stay. Besides," he went on, grinning as a wind up, "I don't think Scorpion would agree as to your going, not yet, and you better pay attention to that horse."

CHAPTER THIRTEEN

AS Tim summed things up he finally got to thinking that Joshua was right. Neither the Trading Post nor big towns would do, and as far as holing up at the wild horse camp and all by himself he agreed with Joshua against that too, it would only be a foolish thing to do, for, as Joshua had said, he couldn't take care of his hurts and he'd be mighty handicapped in doing anything, besides being lonesome, hurting Jane and himself and to no advantage only that if he was away she would maybe forget in time, and he might too, some.

But he wouldn't make up his mind to stay, and he wouldn't dare think of asking Jane to be his wife, not while he was wanted, for it sure wouldn't be fair to her. It wouldn't be the right thing to do in any way.

So he finally decided to "bear along as long as he could," until spring anyhow. Be frank with Jane and have a good understanding with her so she wouldn't be having no false hopes, then when spring come and he was fit to ride again he could start on his trip north as he'd planned. That would be all understood with Jane and maybe work out well enough. And Scorpion wouldn't lay him down when he'd be ready to go the next time, regardless if he was Destiny, Providence or anything else.

That decided on, the snow now all gone and a nice day come when he could be outside and walk around he took Jane's arm and the two went for a walk, past the garden and on to the rim of the big canyon. He didn't say anything much along the way only to remark, like when going by the garden, that in another month or so it ought to be time to start planting things there. Jane would only agree, her mind altogether on what that walk meant. He'd never took her out walking that way before and she was anxious to know what it was all about, having only a small hunch.

He didn't keep her waiting long. The two got to the top of the rim overlooking the canyon, and sitting down on a green patch of creeping cedar, he came to the top with what all had most been on his mind and seemed like for so long.

Putting his hand on hers, he says, "There's only one way of telling with words, I guess. Maybe you already know, but anyway I'm saying that I love you, Jane. I love you with all my heart."

Jane looked at him, more confused than surprised. But there was only one way of her telling with words too, and she finally managed to say, like repeating, "I love you too, Jerry, and with all my heart."

"And you would marry me?" he asks.

"Yes, Jerry. I would be very happy to marry you."

Tim drawed his hand away, looked into the deep of the canyon and blue haze there and he muttered low. "Dammit all, anyhow."

Jane was more than surprised at that and her happy smile vanished as she looked at him, concerned and wondering.

He'd never took her out walking that way before

He finally turned to face her and says: "I'd better come out with it, and I'm so doggone sorry, Jane, but I wish for your own happiness that you didn't care, because I could never ask you to be my wife, not until——"

Then seeing the sudden hurt look come into her eyes, he turned to stare down into the deep of the canyon again and painfully went on to tell her of the reason why, of the happening to the north which stood between 'em. He told it to her the same as he had to Joshua and in as few words as he could, and like with Joshua he felt as safe in telling her as he did him. For that matter, he felt safe towards the whole family that way, for none was of the kind whose brains had been narrowed by narrow ruts. Honesty and trueness was their religion and they gave little thought to man made laws. They could see on both sides of 'em and wouldn't condemn according.

As Tim went on with the telling of the happening, Jane's concern and hurt gradually eased, and instead of giving up she was even made a little happy, happy at the thought that now was something threatening and which they could stand shoulder to shoulder against. She could be of some help to him, and at the thought of that, she only found more happiness.

She looked at the mix-up he'd got into in the same way her father had. She'd seen and knew outlaws too, and like her father, realized that there was outlaws and outlaws, that a price on a man's head doesn't necessarily make him an outlaw, and even tho she felt that

Tim was sure enough reckless, jumping into things before looking and all such, she knew he was no outlaw. His respect, frankness, and squareness towards her, and all he proved himself to be since he come to the ranch more than satisfied her as to that.

Tim didn't see the relieved and happy smile returning to her face as he talked on. He kept a-staring down the canyon. When thru with the telling of the happening he went on with how hopeless he thought it was of his ever getting cleared and exonerated of the mix-up, and how with that hanging over his head he couldn't think of marrying and making a home. For his wife would have to share under the always threatening shadow and suffer along as much as himself if ever the law caught up with him. Even if not, the shadow would always be there over them. That's why he'd been and still was anxious to leave, he told her, before each cared so much for the other. Now it would be mighty hard to do, and unless she would be game and play her part by being just friends he would have to leave as soon as he possibly could. He would leave by spring anyway, and that was certain.

"I can't tell you how sorry I am, Jane, about all of this," he says. "You wouldn't have no use for my kind anyhow, and I should of told you before, but——"

He'd turned to look at her and stopped short. It was now his turn to look surprised and wondering, for Jane was only smiling her prettiest at him and that took all further talk out of him. Here he'd figured she'd been feeling disappointed and hurt all the while he told her, and instead she only seemed happy again, even happier with her confidence in him for his telling her, also by seeing a way of helping him.

At the surprised and unbelieving expressions on his face, Jane's smile went into a little cheerful laugh. She apologized for it at such a time. "But," she says, now more serious, "I thought and was expecting to hear something real dreadful, like your being already married and having a family for instance, or really committing a very serious crime, and the relief of knowing that what you just told me is all there is, . . . why I just had to laugh, Jerry."

Tim had to laugh a little at that too, but it was a kind of a feeling foolish laugh, like as tho he was a child and making something big out of what was really little. He didn't say no more, just gazed down into the canyon again, thinking.

After a while, and with a quiet, sort of soothing voice, Jane begin to speak. She would be game, she said, and play her part, if that's what he wished. She understood. But she would be very happy, much happier to take the chance with him, as his wife and standing by him against what was threatening.

Tim's thoughtful but mighty appreciative look didn't give her any hope there but she went on, game, even if to lose. She went on to tell him of her plans, and as he listened close he had to hide a grin, for if it hadn't been for the sound of her voice and seeing her at the corner of his eye he'd of swore it was Joshua talking. Her plans was so close to the ones Joshua had spread before him some few evenings past that he suspicioned he'd told her, the only difference was that she wasn't for waiting for no year or so, just a reasonable time, if he wished. But with his staying at the ranch and all, her plans tallied up so close to Joshua's that they might of been his.

As she talked on, Tim begin to fear that the plans he'd made as regards to their being just friends would soon topple over, they wouldn't work. He'd already weakened himself, and right now, Jane wasn't playing her part, for she was willing to take the chance, any time.

When she got thru talking, Tim stargazed on for a spell, then sort of shaking himself he stood up. Jane stood up too, and both facing one another Tim says:

"It's no use, Jane. We have to face the fact that we can never marry, and you be game and play your part or I will have to hit out. The sooner we realize there's no hope and set our minds to that the better it will be."

Tim sure meant what he'd just said and it'd been mighty hard for him to say it. Jane had listened quiet, looking straight at him, and only acted sort of resigned like. It surprised Tim that there was no show of sad feelings.

"I'll be game and play my part, Jerry," she says. Then, like to make double sure, "But you will stay?"

"Well, that will be a couple of months yet, and in that time who can tell what may come? You know, while there's life there's hope."

What was back of that and her actions Tim couldn't

guess, but whatever it was sort of wasn't with the agreement just made. He figured right then that it'd be one sided and seen where he'd have to use all of his will power, be firm and make her toe the line as much as he could, reminding her. But as they started back down off the rim and she slipped her little hand into his he only squeezed it. He wasn't quite ready to be firm right yet.

It was a few evenings later when as Joshua came to his tent as usual he spoke up and told him.

"I'm lost, old timer. I'm a gone goslin."

"Why, is it that bad?" grins Joshua.

"Yes, and I've just got to hit out before it gets worse. I'm going to hit out even if I have to hoof it."

Joshua grinned some more. "Providence don't use only horses in making a feller do what she cuts out for him to do," he says. "That old lady always has her way, and I'm not doing any such prophesying but she might roll a boulder on you as you're hoofing it, and lay you down that way. She seems to take a lot of pains with you."

"Yes, and gives me a lot of pains too."

"But laying all jokes to side now, Jerry. I think you're a daggone fool for wanting to get away from here and Jane. You both care for one another as neither of you will ever care for any other. Your going will only bring you both grief, a lifetime of it if you stay apart, for if I'm any kind of a judge, both of you will keep on a-pining and neither of you will ever forget.

"Why don't you make up your mind to do as I said, wait for a year or so till things are forgotten and then if nothing happens to prevent it take a chance? You know, it's part of life for two joined for life to expect some grief, to share and share alike, the bitter with the sweet and thru thick and thin."

"Them words and sentiments are all right," says Tim, "but I don't like the bitter and the thin and the grief part, not for Jane. No, Joshua, I'm afraid there'd be too much of that to drag her into and expect her to share. I think too daggone much of her for that. My trail ahead is mighty rocky, full of snags and too crooked and narrow for two.

"Some little grief has got to be expected, of course," he went on, "but I don't see nothing little in the heavy clouds that's hanging over me in that way, and if I was to dance a jig at the end of a rope with the ground out of reach of my feet why that'd be more than grief, and I'd sure want to be *alone* at the time."

"Why, Jerry," says Joshua, looking a little worried, "they couldn't do that to you."

"It ain't what they can't do, it's what they do do. . . . If it was just the money I could return that and maybe get off easy, then I *might* take a chance. I said I might, but I'm thinking I wouldn't, not until it was all over with. But with the killing them punks pinned on me, that's mighty serious and I sure won't take a chance while that's hovering."

As Joshua had once agreed, while him and Tim had been mending the cedar fence some time back, he finally come to agree with him again this time, that it would be best for him to leave, after all, but to stay as long as he could and at least until he got well. It was a sort of sad looking old mustanger that walked out of the tent that evening.

A couple more weeks went by with Tim and Jane "playing their parts." Jane played her part fairly well, only them eyes of hers sure done a lot of yanking on Tim's heart strings at times. Then he'd have to remind her, which didn't help any. She didn't seem worried about her end of the agreement, that he'd be leaving for certain and there was no hopes and all such, she just was happy he was around and seldom beyond hearing distance.

Then one day and while Tim was more than fretting about what all he was sure the goings on would lead to, an old rider came to the door, and with a "Howdy folks?" walked into the house. It was Old Man Walters from down canyon country.

It was late afternoon and he stayed for supper, and during the talk of the evening, Tim's ears perked up as the old feller was heard to say that he'd rode over to see if he could get either Joshua or Jake to come and help him run in a bunch of his horses. They'd got pretty wild and he would have to have one man help him.

Joshua hadn't been coming along to the tent with Tim the last few days, for Tim was now recuperated well enough so he needed no care. But that evening he asked him to come over with him, and there he told him. He told him he'd be leaving in the morning, with him and old Walters.

Joshua only nodded, and to Tim's surprise, he even seemed pleased. "I guess it will be a relief for me to go," he thought to himself. But, come to think of it now, he'd noticed a queer and satisfied look that came to Joshua's face one day, a week or so before, replacing the downhearted look he'd been packing and the cheerful one had come to stay, like something had been stirred, settled, and all to the good.

He was surprised some more when the next morning he told 'em all he was leaving and none hung their heads nor seemed sad. Little Margie didn't give no hint of a whimper, and even Jane took the news kind of easy, like set to play her part. Too much that way, he figured, and that all more than got him to wondering, feeling a little hurt. Maybe they was all glad to get rid of him by now.

But his feelings was eased a considerable as after he'd said "good bye" to all once more and started to the corrals Jane took a holt of his free arm and went along with him. He was all puzzled and tried hard to think of what horse he was to ride, a gentle horse which Joshua had told him he should take. But going into the corral, Jane left him at the gate, and to his wonder and unbelieving eyes, she walked straight to Scorpion who stood plum still as she slipped the hackamore on his head, led him out and went to saddling him. It would of been near impossible for Tim to put his saddle on Scorpion with only his left hand.

It was Old Man Walters from down canyon country

Scorpion stood and acted as gentle as an old barn raised plow horse as Jane saddled him, and when Joshua and old Walters passed by to saddle their horses, Joshua had to grin at Tim and remark about Jane and Scorpion as he went on.

"What did I tell you?" he says.

The saddling done and Tim now ready to go, Jane, holding on to the bridle reins, turned to face him. She didn't look so brave as a little while before and her voice sort of trembled as she spoke.

"Now, Tim," she says, trying mighty hard not to show her feelings, "being that you're bound to go, will you do me a big favor and promise me one thing?"

"Why, I guess so, Jane, if it's possible."

"It's possible, and only that you go with Mr. Walters and that you stay with him for at least a month. If you won't promise me that I can't let you have this horse. But you will promise me that, won't you? I want to have you get well before you go on, Jerry, that's all."

But there was more to it than that, Tim felt, as he seen how anxious she was to have him promise, and whatever it was he couldn't guess. The promise was easy enough, and it was just what he'd planned to do, to stay with old Walters until he was well enough to ride on.

"I'll sure promise you that, Jane," he says, taking both her hands in his (his right hand had been out of the bandage for a week now, just to the wrist). "I'd planned to do that very same thing, and it will be a great consolation to me, and you too I hope, that I'm not so far away from you while my hurts heal, and the biggest hurt, the one of having to leave you and which will never heal, sort of numbs and the sharpest edges blunt some.

"The only thing is," he went on, "I don't know if Mr. Walters would let me stay so long. I'd of course pay my board and all that, but you know how some of them old lone wolves are. Then again, I might be found out there and run in. Them's the only things that'd make me break my promise."

Jane smiled a little. "Well, then, I won't have to worry," she says, "and you won't have to worry either, dear, because I know Mr. Walters would be very pleased to have your good company. He's been very lonely since his wife died and his family married and left him. As for the law, I think you'll be nearly as safe there as here." She kissed him on the cheek.

He kissed her too, and not on the cheek, and holding her close he says: "I'm going to say good bye now, Jane, but somehow I feel it's not going to be good bye. Maybe it's because I won't be so far away for a while. But it is good bye, Jane."

He kissed her again, then turning away he went to get on Scorpion who only quivered a little as he eased himself into the saddle, and he rode away to catch up with Joshua and old Walters.

CHAPTER FOURTEEN

BUT what seemed a miracle to Tim, Scorpion didn't make one false move on the forty mile ride to old Walters' ranch. He got off and back on him again a couple of times during that ride, and even tho he'd been kind of awkward in doing that each time, with the use of only his left arm, the horse had even been patient with him and stood stock still while he got on.

"Not like the last time when you tried to ride him away from the ranch, is he?" remarks Joshua as the three rode along.

"Can't make him out," was all Tim could say.

"Why, that's easy. You're just riding along the trail Destiny has marked out for you, that's all. A fairy come along, touched him with her magic stick and that quick he's no bronc no more."

Tim grinned. "You mean Jane, don't you? . . . I've never had him act so good before, no time, and now it's been over a month since I rode him. She sure must have a magic touch all right. And talking about your Destiny," he went on, "and that he safely packed me on the long trip only to dump me near your place, he didn't make it very safe for me then, I had to do some tall scrambling many times on the long trip before I got to your place and had to put on a lot of action to keep him from getting me a few times when he sure enough tried to."

"It was only the bronc in him then and that had to come out. But now he's even more dangerous that it's out, for he's all to see that you toe the mark as Destiny has set it for you. He's your horse of Destiny for sure."

Old Walters, who'd been riding by Joshua's side, finally had to bust loose at such talk. "What nonsense are you jabbering about anyhow, Joshua?" he asks.

"No nonsense at all," says Joshua, and then he went on to tell him of the peculiar ways and the facts about the chestnut. He of course didn't mention where Tim started from nor give any hint as to why or what such actions might be leading to, only that it was leading to something to the good and which Tim would sooner or later find out. Joshua himself couldn't guess but he felt that way about it.

Old Walters looked past Joshua at Tim and both grinned at one another. "Do you believe all that diluded prune juice?" he asks.

Tim only shrugged one shoulder. "Doggone if I know what to think," he says. "This horse has played me enough tricks that way that sometimes I do think Joshua is halfways right."

Old Walters looked at Scorpion's head. "Well," he says.

"You're durn tooting I'm halfways right," Joshua went on, "and then some. You'll find out if you try to ride him away and start out for where you shouldn't."

"I wouldn't have no such a horse," says old Walters. "Not unless he could talk and let me know in advance what the samhill I should do and where I should go, and even then I wouldn't want no such a horse."

"But now," Joshua says, paying no attention to the remark. He pointed a thumb at Tim. "This boy here, he would like to stay with you till he heals up and is well enough to ride again. Could you put him up, say for about a month or so?"

Old Walters' eyes lit up in pleasure. "Why ask such fool questions?" he says. "You know durn well I'd be mighty glad to put him up and for as long as he wants to stay." Then squinting at Tim, he asks: "Can you play checkers, or dominoes or pinochle, young feller?"

Tim shook his head. "No," he says, "but everybody tells me I'm smart and I guess I can learn." Being called a boy and a young feller kind of surprised him and he thought he'd answer back that way.

"He's not only smart," Joshua added on, "but he's good looking too. At least that's what my daughter Jane tells me. Yep, and she's the reason why he's not staying with us any longer, because him and her done went and fell in love with one another."

"That's a kind of a queer reason for him to hit out, ain't it?" says old Walters.

Tim squirmed in his saddle and tried to change the subject by doing some talking too, but it didn't work, and then realizing that there should be some excuse why he didn't stay at Joshua's and then seeing that Joshua would have his own way of giving the reason by simply telling the truth in his joking way, he suffered along as best he could.

"Yes," Joshua was going on. "He's got the idea his trail is too rough for a woman and that he should hit it by his lonesome. So, fearing that his affections would finally get the best of him and he'd weaken, he figured it safest to get away. But he sure ain't in no shape to ride and that's why he'd better stay with you till he's well. And don't you let him get away for at least a month. Being hurt the way he is and then love-sick to boot is mighty hard on the boy, and he ought to stay two months by rights."

"I'll try and hold him as long as I can," says old Walters, "and I can doctor up his body hurts too, but as far as his love-sickness I don't know what to do about that, unless maybe he gets to learn how to play checkers and pinochle. That's sort of good for a feller's mind, occupies it and drives away lonesomeness and hankerings. I've been playing solitaire for going on fifteen years now and I'm beginning to get tired of it."

It was near dark when they come to sight of the ranch, and even with the sunlight and shadows gone, Tim thought as he looked the country over, the good sized meadow below the rim, the big trees and the setting of the house, stables, other buildings and corrals that he'd never seen a place as pretty and more to his liking, more than topping the description Joshua had given him of it.

Unsaddling at the stable and turning the horses in the meadow the three men walked up to a higher level where the house stood on a patch of lawn and amongst a few big cottonwood trees. They would throw a good

He'd never seen a place as pretty and more to his liking

shade, thought Tim, sizing 'em up natural like and for he didn't know why, and they wouldn't cut off any view either nor make the house dark, for there wasn't too many of 'em and the heavy limbs branched out at a good height.

Walking into the big kitchen, old Walters soon had a fire started and the kettle begin to sing. The heat felt good, for the days was still plenty cool and the nights cold. All pleased with company around, old Walters went to stirring a batch of sourdough for biscuits, remarking the while that it seemed queer to be talking and realizing he was being heard, and how he'd have to be careful of what he'd say now, for he'd been talking to himself and empty space for so long that he'd got careless that way.

"Nobody's been here since last fall," he says, as he went on molding the biscuits with his hands. "It was a couple of fellers in a automobile and come up here to hunt deer for a few days. They got three bucks and left me one, and that meat lasted me all winter. That's still some of it you're cutting on now," he says to Joshua, who'd got busy. "It sure lasts good in the spring house where I keep it. That spring house being in the shade against the rim and covered with moss and brush, the way it is, snow piling up on it and staying till near summer, fresh meat keeps good as well and better than in an ice box even in hot summer days."

Joshua, glancing at Tim, who was doing his best at peeling potatoes, remarked: "You'll have to get used to his raving about that spring house of his, Jerry, and about other things on this place of his, and you'll have to agree with him too and listen or he'll have cat fits."

"Yeh," old Walters snorted. "It just hurts you that you haven't got such a spring house, you old fuzztail hunter, or such a place as I've got." Then he grinned. "And if I remember right I wasn't far ahead of you when I got it. A couple of days late and it'd be yours instead of mine. Ain't that right, Joshua?"

"That's right," Joshua had to agree, "and remember the cussing I gave you for being here first?" he added on, laughing.

"I sure do, and you been cussing me ever since. But," old Walters went on, acting serious, "I guess it was Destiny that I should have it, even if I was riding a wagon at the time."

The two old timers went on reminiscing as the late supper was being cooked, and they argued on good natured thru the meal that way and about the goings of the "early days."

But, the dishes washed and put away, it wasn't long afterwards when a last cigarette was rolled for the day. Old Walters stood up and stretched, and pointing to a door told Tim to make himself comfortable in the room there. Joshua and him went to another room.

Being still a little weak, the forty mile ride of that day soon put Tim to sleep. The breaking away from Jane hadn't hit him full force as yet, and it wasn't till daybreak the next morning that it begin. But then, as it got lighter and he got to surveying the room that sort of drawed his interest to where he near felt contented. He wouldn't let himself think of her or that he wouldn't see her no more, and he put his attention to the room as he layed there on the big soft bed, an oak bed that had been in old Walters' family for many years.

The room was cheerful and bright, light and plastered smooth over the thick adobe walls. There was a few colorful old time pictures in dark frames and some family portraits, a "chimayo" hung like as a tapestry, adding on plenty more color and which jibed well with the navajos on the dark stained floor of wide boards. In one corner was a fireplace, and with the couple of pieces of furniture that went to furnish the room, Tim thought it was as pretty a room as he'd ever slept into.

But he didn't get to do much surveying of it that first and early morning, for it hadn't got light enough to see too well when he heard the rattling of stove lids in the kitchen, then he got up and dressed and went to join the two older men. They was again beginning to argue, this time about horses.

"Why, I sure wouldn't sell that stud bunch," Joshua was saying. "It's the best horse and bunch you've got."

"That's just the reason why I want to sell it," answers old Walters, "before anybody steals it. It's the first bunch that'd be run off and I'm not going to take any chances."

Tim wondered about the talk and more about the horses. It went on thru the breakfast of bacon and potatoes, plenty of coffee and more fresh sourdough biscuits. Tim asked if they'd need him to help run in the horses, and getting a quick answer from the two that he wasn't needed he went on to say that he'd have plenty of time and would wash the dishes, get in some kindling and wood and straighten things up in general while they was gone.

"And take it easy," old Walters added on.

That sounded like Joshua, thought Tim. But, as he come to think of it later, they was both from the same country, Kentucky, and maybe from the same county and where, as Tim got to learn, they'd both been "carted" from when they was two-year-olds that accounted for it. Old Walters' folks had hit for New Mexico many years before Joshua's folks started. Joshua's folks hit for Texas, and it wasn't until the two growed up and drifted away and then met along the canyon rim that they knew they'd been born in the same state, Kentucky, and maybe in the same county. They'd never learned the name of the county, only that, as they'd often heard their paps say, mighty good ponies was raised there, and on that one point they both always agreed. That's what Old Walters' stock originated from.

Leaving the dishes to Tim and telling him "they'd keep," the two old riders started down for the corral where one old horse was always kept up and rode only to bring in fresh horses. Tim grinned as he watched 'em. Old Walters, eighty years old, Joshua, sixty, and both acting like twenty. They argued on about horses as they went, one for selling and the other for holding

They argued on about horses as they went

and they disappeared into the corrals and out of Tim's sight that way.

Tim's mind wasn't much on the dishes as he went on to gathering and washing 'em, then "mucked" out the kitchen which, as he noticed, had been kept mighty clean. As he "took it easy" and worked at that he kept a-thinking about the horses, of old Walters wanting to sell his best stud bunch, and somehow or other he didn't want him to sell them either, and somehow or other again, Jane seemed to come in his thoughts with them, like agreeing with him and Joshua. He would see what kind of horses they was.

His work done in the kitchen, he straightened up his bed and went outside to get some wood. He would have to keep the fire going, for there was a stew on. It was a cool, clear and bright day, such a day as don't allow any suffering of any kind.

An early sun, along with the song of a meadow lark greeted him as he blinked at all the brightness around him, and, if only Jane was near, he could hear her sing too.

At the neat and stacked up wood pile of mesquite, piñon and juniper mixed, all cut to stove lengths and chopped, Tim didn't see where he'd only have to pack some in. There was plenty of good bark for kindling and that'd be easy to gather. So he didn't see nothing much to do but just mosey around and sort of look the place over. For as Joshua had arranged it for him it would be his home for a month or so, or, as old Walters had said, as long as he wanted to stay, and he'd as well get acquainted with it. He would have plenty of time before the horses was brought in.

He begin with the house, and circling around it now in the bright daylight he got to see and appreciate what a pretty setting it was in, and the build of the house itself. It was of adobe, the walls four feet thick, plastered of adobe outside and whitewashed. The roof was of Jack pine limbs, topped with corrugated iron and many inches of red shale holding it down, making the house cool in summer and warm in winter. No bullets nor weather could penetrate it.

Four rooms went to make up the house, all in a straight line and with a door from each room out to a wide porch. Tim seen where there'd been flowers and vines by that porch and around the house, and looking at 'em he figured some would grow again soon as spring come and frost was out of the ground.

He went to the spring house then, old Walters' pride, and even tho he seen that no better place could be found for one, he also seen that it hadn't been used much for some years. But empty milk pans was stacked on empty milk shelves. There was crocks and a churn in one corner, a meat block and all that was necessary for the keeping of a home in fresh butter, milk and meat and vegetables, but all there was in sight in that line was a small deer loin on the meat block and part of a slab of bacon on a milk shelf, but no milk nor no butter or vegetables, only half a sack of potatoes.

Tim grinned at the scarcity there. Sure enough a fine spring house, he thought, but mighty little stored in it as to what there ought to be. All proof that old Walters wasn't much of a hand at milking cows and gardening.

From there he moseyed on down to the corrals and stable, all in a good location and where the waters would quickly drain away from, all to soon dry. The corrals wasn't in very good shape, neither was the stable, made of stone and which wasn't much more than a shed. But the winters being sort of mild in that country there wasn't much use for a warm stable. Stock done better free anyway, and there was plenty of good shelter when needed.

There was a chicken house and pig pen and Tim had to grin some more at seeing how long they'd been empty. Old Walters wasn't much for chores or any kind of manual labor either, he thought. All had been in good shape and running full swing once, he could see that, and now he could also see that with the good location it all was spread on it wouldn't be much work to put everything into shape and running full swing again. There was a good clear stream running thru one corner of the big square corral and that was fine. Nothing like good spring water running thru a feed corral.

But if the corrals, all but the round one, and stable and other little buildings had been sort of neglected and run down there, the house sure hadn't. Tim could see from where he was that it sure had been taken care of, like for in memory of the family raised there, and it wouldn't need no repairs. With it, the location and all in general, the country surrounding Tim thought it was as close to paradise as anything earthly could come to.

He seen that the main corral gate was well opened, that nothing was in the wings leading to it which would spook the horses brought in, and then walked on up to the house again. He stirred the fire, added on more wood to keep the stew simmering and then he went out on the wide porch and sat on a big and heavy home-hewed chair there.

With the solid and homey house at his back and all that was before and around him Tim thought it would be mighty pleasant to live a life time and grow old in such a place and country, *if only*. . . . That "if" near got the best of him with the thought of what all stood between him and ever being able to enjoy this which he wanted the most. What would even this be without Jane to share and enjoy with him?

It took him a long time to get his mind off the subject, and Jane. He wondered how she felt now that he'd left, and he could near vision her in the blue of the deep canyon below, the same blue and the same deep canyon which she might be looking into now. But such thoughts wouldn't do, and Tim didn't let his sight linger there. Then looking along the rims and over 'em a tall and soaring cloud of dust attracted his attention. It was against the hills from the canyon and at the sight he knew it was the horses coming, many miles away yet but they was coming, old Walters and Joshua hazing 'em.

CHAPTER FIFTEEN

THE sun was high and well past noon when at a break in the canyon rim and like as a chute into the main corral, Tim seen the bunch of horses come to sight against the sky line. A rider leading 'em dropped back at the rim and fell in behind 'em with the other rider, then an old mare took the lead and in a short while the whole bunch, stud and all, was in the corral.

Tim didn't start down to the corrals at the sight. Instead he went into the kitchen, put more wood in the stove to get the oven hot, and seeing the stew of venison, rice and potatoes was well done, set it back to where it'd keep hot. He didn't dare start the biscuits because he'd long ago learned how finicky old sourdoughs was with their sourdough. Nobody could handle it but their perticular selves.

So, knowing they'd be hungry and that no time would be spent at the corrals until the late noon meal was over with, he done his next best and went to setting the table with all the necessaries to eat with, spices, peppers, sweetening and all.

He'd got that well done and all set when the sound of the two old mustangers' spurs came to his ears. Old Walters busted in with a cheerful "Hello, son" to Tim, but otherwise acting as mad as a wolf that'd bumped into a porcupine.

He set his hat back off his sweated forehead, and pointing a thumb at Joshua who, winking at Tim, was trailing close behind, he says, "I'll be a dingbusted sheep herder and lousy to boot before I ever ask that hide bound, sunburnt shade hunter to run horses with me again."

Tim, being wise to the two, didn't say a word. He only acted interested and so old Walters wouldn't "have a cat fit."

"Why, goldurn and be danged," he went on. "I was running horses in old New Mexico and growed whiskers before he ever let out his first beller, and here he rides along with me and keeps a trying to tell *me* what *I* should do with *my* ponies——"

Getting no backfire, old Walters finally took off his hat at the all set table and whiff of the stew. Then rolling up his sleeves, washing his hands and appreciating the fact that his sourdough crock hadn't been disturbed, he got good natured and plum forgot what more he was going to say, and started to mix the bread.

There was nothing for Joshua to do right then excepting wash his own hands and prepare to eat, and while doing that he had to remark: "It ain't how long ago a feller has been born nor how long he lives, it's how much he's got the brains to learn and gets to know."

That dart went blunt against old Walters' now happy mind. The sight of Tim, and thought of his company, made him feel that way, and he answered the way he felt, still pointing at Joshua as a arch enemy but with a smile.

At a break in the canyon rim and like as a chute into the main corral, Tim seen the bunch of horses come to sight against the sky line

"Why, that old lizard," he says to Tim while greasing a bread pan, "he never layed an eye on a good horse till I got some in the country, and do you know, Jerry, he's been after me for nigh on some forty years a trying to tell me how I should run 'em (raise them) and do with 'em——"

Joshua tried to squeeze in a word there but it only wound up in a grin. For there was no space for any word to be edged in as old Walters went right on.

"And all the time I was riding with him since morning, all I got from that 'youngster' was advice that I shouldn't sell that stud bunch we brought in. I say *we* brought in but it was only me, because he was of no use, always doing nothing but bellering that I was this or that for even thinking of selling them horses. That's all he done and all the help I got from him all morning along, and when he wasn't jabbering that way he rested on his cantle and horse's kidneys. I had to do the hazing and the turning of the ponies while he just bored holes in his horse's back and moped. He didn't want nothing to do with me selling them ponies, and son," he says to Tim as he stuck a pan of warmed dough into the hot oven, "I've got a stinking hunch he just hopes my stuff gets to running wild so's he can get 'em. He's sure short of good saddle stock, I know."

There was no comeback from Joshua. He was only looking down towards the horses in the corral and didn't seem to be hearing any of what old Walters was saying. His look and thoughts was only for the horses there, and Tim catching him at that, understood. It all tallied up with the way he felt.

The late noon meal was spread and all went to it only to enjoy it while thinking and talking, of horses. And with that it was some time before the meal was over. Then a pot and skillet was put away, "the dishes would keep," and all started down for the corral.

Tim was near the first there, and glimpsing at the heads, then to the clean limbs of the swift built horses he squinted to Joshua like as much as to say it was "no sale" for them horses. Old Walters was close third into the corral, and all three a-standing there, sizing up points and none seeing any defects made old Walters all the happier and prouder, then near to tears with the thought of parting with 'em.

"And, dadburn my hide," he says. "I've got to part with 'em now, after all my babying 'em."

"They're not bad horses to look at," says Joshua, sort of sarcastic and to keep old Walters from getting too sentimental or to thinking he had to part with 'em. "I don't know as I'd want one of 'em if I was to go a ways."

That remark done the work, and old Walters more than bristled up at hearing it. He then went to praising his horses till there was no end to it and downing Joshua's at the same time. All the while Joshua walked around the corral, looking them over well and not seeming to hear. Then getting too far to holler at, old Walters turned to Tim, who'd stood by and kept watching the horses, going on telling some more about their merits to him.

Tim agreed with all he said about 'em, for they was sure enough good horses and that more than pleased old Walters, and after he'd slowed down some, Tim says:

"That's just it, Mister Walters——"

"Never mind the Mister, Jerry," he interrupts there. "It sounds like you're trying to sell me something. Just call me Walt or anything short."

"All right, Walt," Tim went on, "but what I was going to say is that them horses are too good to sell out as stock horses and in a bunch that way. They ought to be gentled a little, halter broke and sold one head at a time at a good market and you'd get four times the money for them."

Old Walters listened close. This cowboy appreciated good horses, talked sense, and that went well with him. Tim went on.

"Them mares with good colts by their side this spring would be worth plenty more. During summer, and after the colts are a few months old, the mares could be halter broke and gentled, sold one at a time, each with a colt, and you can guess for yourself how much more they'd bring."

Old Walters pondered a while. Tim was sure right. "But," he says, "I expect a buyer to take 'em tomorrow or next day."

"Set a price?" asks Tim.

"Yes, fifty dollars a head straight thru."

"Why that's giving 'em away. I'd rather see 'em stole than let 'em go for that price. Them mares, sold as I said and with a colt by their side, would bring four times that much this fall, and worth a lot more if you took your time selling 'em. If I was you I'd sure get out of that deal by just saying that you want $200 a head for them. They're worth that and if the buyer wants to pay the price you're not loser, if he don't you're still not loser."

Surprised at such a price, old Walters scratched his head, more than pleased at the way Tim valued the horses. He was right, he thought, "but."

"The only thing is," he says, "the riding after them horses, keeping track of 'em and seeing that nobody drifting thru in a hurry gets away with 'em. I'm too old to do that any more, let alone halter breaking and gentling 'em, and I don't know of a soul I can trust doing that for me unless it's Joshua, but he's getting too old too and plenty busy on his own place. Besides, I want to sell out, get away from here as quick as I can and be with my daughter for my last few years."

Before Tim realized and thought, he put his foot in it by saying: "I'll take care of your horses, gentle 'em and sell 'em for you, and I ought to be able to start in doing that in another month."

At them words, old Walters acted as tho he'd been standing by a gold mine and hadn't discovered it till just then. His face lit up, all smiles, and he let out

Them mares with good colts by their side this spring would be worth plenty more

a holler that spooked the horses to near running over Joshua on the other side.

"By geeminy Christmas!" he says, coming near slapping Tim's bum shoulder. "I sure never thought of that." Then squinting at Tim and anxious, "But will you be staying here with me that long, son? It'll be late summer by then, you know."

There was no backing out now. But thinking it over and wondering about why and wherefore his interest in the horses, Tim finally just said, "Yes, Walt. I'll take care of them horses."

* * *

"That's how come when the horse buyer drove up in his car the next day he started back for town near as quick as he came, all in a huff and without ever looking at the horses, for old Walters had set his price up to $200 a head for them. "Who'd ever heard of such a price for range bred horses and in that country?" the buyer had said. To which old Walters had answered that he was hearing of it now.

But that all sort of left Tim in a pickle, and even tho he knew that old Walters wouldn't expect him to get such a price for the horses, he'd expect a heap more than fifty dollars a head and to stay till the horses was sold. That's what old Walters wanted the most, for Tim to stay, and now, with him to take care of 'em he wouldn't be in no hurry to part with 'em. Tim seen where he'd sure enough tied himself to stay at old Walters' for most of the summer, and he'd have to put off his trip to the north until that time instead of by spring as he'd planned.

That part didn't bother him much. That trip could wait and the cached money would also keep until he could well make the trip. He'd be in good shape again by that time. What worried him the most was that he would be so close to Jane and for so long after he'd be able to travel on, and with the parting with her the way he did that's what he'd wanted to do, travel on. Then there was the chances he'd be taking of officers or others who might drop in at the ranch and identify him with the reward.

It was a foolish thing he'd done, he thought, and it puzzled him as he'd said he would stay that he'd said the words as tho he had no control of 'em, like they just flew out of him, unthinking. Something like when he'd jumped off the train to the north and held up the bandits.

But there was no undoing of what had already been done, nor taking back the words that had been said. He would now have to put up with it, suffer along, take the chances "and see what come of it."

Old Joshua, along with old Walters, was mighty pleased to hear of his staying and taking care of the stock. In another month or so he could start in doing that, and then old Walters' worries about his horses and cattle would be over. Joshua vouched for that.

The horses was drove out of the meadow and left to go back to their range a short while after the buyer came and went. It was still early in the day, and

Joshua started back for home, saying to Tim that he felt happy now he wouldn't be so far away, for him to ride up and visit when he could and drag old "whiskers" along. His last laughing remark as he rode away was, "Just imagine him a-trying to sell them slab-sided, spindle-legged horses of his for two hundred a head. Why, I've caught many fuzztails as good as them and felt mighty lucky to get ten dollars a head."

Old Walters, standing by Tim, only laughed back at that and didn't answer, and afterwards he only said, "I always let him have the last word. It makes him feel good, and he'd get it anyway."

The regular life of the ranch went on from that day. There was nothing much that Tim could do only as he'd done the first day and that didn't take much of his time. Old Walters would be riding some most every day, and other times just puttering around the ranch but not at anything where Tim could help. Besides he was told that he wasn't wanted to do anything, only maybe walk around a little but to take it as easy as he could so he'd heal up well and quick.

Old Walters doctored him up and renewed the bandages now and again, and after some few days he got him so he could play a fair hand of pinochle and make himself hard to corner at checkers. Some hours was spent that way most every day and that helped break the monotony for Tim. But being used to plenty of action he craved more for that than any time in his life. He was also more lonely than any time he could remember of, and even tho more at ease and his longing feelings for Jane relieved by her not being in sight or near, he all the time felt more lonely for her, seemed like more and more every day, and the old saying of "Absence makes the heart grow fonder" sure struck home with him.

The one great satisfaction he had, even tho the yearning with it was hard to endure at times, was that she wasn't so far away and he could ride over and see her if he wished. He'd of course never do that but he had that satisfaction anyway. Another was the beauty of the ranch which, seemed like every day, showed itself more pretty. The grass on the lawn and meadow was fast beginning to green, the trees begin to bud. The birds and their song was everywhere, and it sometimes was very peaceful to just sit on the porch and take on Mother Nature's wonders at their best. If them thoughts of his would only behave and stay put and if he wasn't sort of tied to a chair, he couldn't of asked for more. As it was, and with his thoughts, he was steady trying to figure a way, a way where somehow Jane and him would share their happiness and this place together.

He knew it was hopeless of course, and he done his best to put it all out of his mind so as to go on thru with what he'd decided. But even when his mind would be most occupied them thoughts stuck mighty close and often came to the top. There was no getting rid of 'em, and he'd go to stargazing even while old Walters talked horses to him, sometimes to making a false move or play at checkers or cards and not moving nor playing when his turn come.

"It must be awful tough on a feller," old Walters would say. "I guess this calf love must be near as serious as the real 'McCoy' and hard to get over with."

There was many ways he would dig at Tim on the subject and which would get him out of his trances, and Tim didn't like to be caught at that either, for that would make him feel as tho he sure enough hadn't growed up as yet.

In a week or so's time, and against old Walters' wishes, Tim started riding. He wouldn't, he said, do any tall hazing of any wild stuff nor try to tail down a cow, but he could get the lay of where the horses and cattle was ranging and keep tab on 'em. A rider's horse tracks that was about the same as posted signs, and the more of 'em there was the more it'd show how the stock was looked after and watched, keeping any wise enough rider drifting thru from shoving a bunch ahead of him as he went.

Tim rode Scorpion, not steady but every other time or so and oftener than only when riding should be done. That little bunch of stock, horses and cattle, wasn't enough to keep a man near busy, but to Tim they was a good excuse to air his mind and they saved him from plain idle riding, which with him would never be thought of to do. Most of old Walters' saddle horses being near or well in the voting age, smooth mouthed and stiff at the joints, wasn't at all what Tim cared to ride. He rode some of them and left Scorpion to feed and rest as much as he could. But there was no resting Scorpion, he'd had a good rest, and his eye was the same as Tim's whenever Tim went to catch another horse.

One day, Tim was riding him thru cedar breaks while getting a tab on the cattle, and looking down the flat below he seen an automobile streaking thru and like heading for the ranch. He watched it, and making sure it turned off the main road and started up the canyon he just sat Scorpion, his heart pounding a little.

He wondered who was in the car and what they was going to the ranch for. He'd always wonder and feel sort of fidgety at any strangers coming to the ranch, and he realized then more than he ever had before that he'd be that way for as long as that reward hung over him. He was too close to such a well travelled road to feel comfortable, specially during the coming summer months.

It was then it came to him that he should be drifting on and to where he'd feel more safe. He'd been at old Walters' for over a month now and he felt recuperated enough to do that. Scorpion had been acting so good and docile that he hardly ever watched him any more and never thought of him as ever repeating the past performances, whether he was a horse of Destiny or what.

He got off of him, and sitting by the shade of a cedar went to studying him while thinking of drifting

It was then it came to him that he should be drifting on

on. He'd of course promised old Walters he'd stay till his horses sold well, but that could be rushed some and a fair price agreed on. That would have to be done before he could feel free to leave, for besides his promise, he felt responsible for old Walters not selling his horses as he would have when the buyer come.

Now he sort of wished he hadn't butted in and had left the sale go on, even if he did believe and know that the horses was worth a heap more than the buyer offered. But it seemed like he was bound to always do such things as jumping before looking. He could be free to go now if it hadn't been for that, and as it was, he was only sitting in the shade of a cedar, wishing he could, and wondering and fidgeting about who all might be in the automobile he'd seen stirring the dust for the ranch.

He hardly dared ride in now to find out, not in plain daylight, and even tho he tried to ease and encourage himself by thinking he was imagining things and was fretting for no reason, he felt a heap more easy where he was than he would by riding into the ranch right then. It would be noon by the time he got there and in time for dinner, but dinner would have to go on without him that day. He'd ride on to locate the horses, and taking his time he would make it back by dark, then he would be on the outside looking into the lighted house and he'd sort of have a first look in and advantage that way.

Noon time went by, and it was away past it when he made his circle, located the two stud bunches and turned back to where he could again see the road that branched out towards the ranch,—just in time too to see an automobile on that road, he figured the same one he'd seen before, and now streaking back out again the direction it had come.

Tim felt mighty relieved at that, and as he watched the car hit the main road and speed on, he let Scorpion amble on at that distance eating fox trot gait of his. He'd be at the ranch in time for supper.

"Well," says old Walters, holding a couple of plates as Tim walked in the house, "I've been kind of worried about you when you didn't show up at noon. Thought maybe you'd started a direction you shouldn't and Scorpion raised Cain about it."

Tim grinned. "I never think about meal times much while I'm riding," he says, "not till the work is done."

"But I wish you'd been here today noon," says old Walters, setting the plates on the table. "There was another horse buyer come,"—his face lit up with a wide smile—"and this one offers me seventy-five dollars a head for my horses. You was sure right, Jerry, when you said they was worth a heap more than fifty, and it looks like the buyers are beginning to realize now that I know it too."

Tim was surprised and pleased. "And what did you say to the offer?" he asks.

"Just told him like what you said, that my price was two hundred per head. But that I might consider a hundred and fifty if the deal was made before the colts come."

"What did he say to that?"

"About the same as the first buyer, only he wasn't so huffy. And, between you and me, I think they'll come to time."

Tim, some disappointed, shook his head. "I'm afraid not," he says. "I've been thinking about it quite a bit lately, and got to figuring that if you got between seventy-five and a hundred dollars per head on 'em you'd be doing fine. I overestimated some when I said two hundred, but that was considering that you'd be seeing to the selling of them yourself, each head separate. That would be taking considerable of your time and expense and you might not be winners in the long run. I think now that you'd be better off selling 'em right here for between seventy-five and a hundred, and maybe that buyer would take 'em then."

It was old Walters' turn to shake his head. "No, sir," he says. "You was right in the first place and I can see it now. I'm going to stick to my price and make them boogers come to time. It took you to make me see how many years I've been cheated and I'm sure thankful to you for that, young feller."

Tim sort of groaned to himself. There'd be no budging him now.

"There was another feller come with that horse buyer too," says old Walters as he pulled the biscuits out of the oven. "This other feller was out to buy my place here. He's come out to do that quite a few times."

Tim's ears perked up at that. "Yeh?" he says.

"Yeh," old Walters went on, "and I'm holding out

on him too, and till he comes to time. I'm sure not going to give it away even if I'm too old and decrepit to take care of it any longer. He offers me only four thousand for it, stock and cellar and all, and my stock alone is worth more than that. Of course, it would be for cash, and that's worth considering some, I think."

For some reason that Tim couldn't figure out, the mention of selling the place sort of hit him between the eyes. He thought it over for a spell and then, acting as natural as he could, he asks:

"And how much are you holding out for, if it's any of my business?"

"Seven thousand," says old Walters, without blinking an eye. Then afterwards he added on, "but I would consider six thousand cash with responsible parties."

"Do you think he'll come to that?"

"He seems anxious, and he might," says old Walters with a satisfied grin.

It was a thoughtful meal for Tim, and he hardly knew what he was eating nor what old Walters was saying as he went thru it. It was after it was over, the dishes done, and the two was outside enjoying the sun's last rays of now longer days, when Tim spoke up on the subject of the horses again, and the selling of the place.

"I guess, after all," he says, "that maybe you're right in holding the price you've set on them horses of yours, and as for the place, I think that with stock and all as it is it's sure worth six thousand, and more."

"You're durn tooting, Jerry," says old Walters, pleased, "and I'm sure glad to have you to help me hold it together till I let go of everything here."

Tim was also sure glad to be there at that time. He didn't know why, nor why he was so interested. But as he went to the dark of his room that evening and layed stretched out on the bed there was more than a hunch come to him as he thought on the subject and the whyfor as to his interest.

He thought and tossed and turned things over in his mind until so late that night that it seemed he'd no more than closed his eyes when he heard the rattling of the stove lids as old Walters started a fire for the breakfast. He layed there a while, gazing at the ceiling and letting simmer back all he'd thought out that night. Then feeling satisfied he got up, feeling all cheerful at what had been thought out, simmered thru and then decided on. He wondered how come he hadn't thought of such a thing before.

CHAPTER SIXTEEN

BEING he'd rode well the day before, all the stock had been accounted for and was running where they belonged, Tim didn't see no use of riding that day, nor the next for that matter. So after breakfast was over with and a little puttering was done outside he hit for his room and closed the door on himself there. It was good that old Walters had saddled up and decided to take a little *pasear* around, for that morning he wanted to be very much in private, all alone with his thoughts of the night before and to carry on what he'd decided to do. What he now figured he should of done long ago.

But better late than never, so with writing pad and pencil and bending over a table he proceeded, he started to writing a letter. He wrote it once, not so many words but it took him an hour, and then tore it up to write it over. The first one had said too much, too much in case somebody else than the one intended for got to reading it. For the letter was intended for Pete, and Pete only.

With his second letter he done his best to make it as much of a riddle as he could in case a stranger got to reading it, but so that Pete could well make sense of it. After it was done it all summed up as much as to say that he was anxious to have the money he'd cached returned to the express company, and that if it would exonerate him he would furnish the thousand he'd took out, he could easy produce that much. For Pete to try and see what he could do for him that way because it was very important that it should be done and as soon as possible.

He wrote to get the "wet stuff" and have it delivered to the company. "Wet stuff" in Border language means cattle or horses that's been swum acrost the Rio Grande and no duty paid, most always stolen stock that meant the money box. As far as "the company" was concerned it could be any kind of company and from bolts to nuts. He went on then with how well he'd done the last *two years with his sheep*, how it helped a lot now that his mother-in-law was staying with 'em, for she could take care of the kids, and his wife could help with the sheep. He wound up that he was doing *fine* and wished Pete could come and visit him, saying he hadn't seen him for many years now. Pete would well see between the lines there, he also would understand when he wrote in a joking way and asked if he was still to blame for the sheep killing up there when he only took a fat mutton. With that he meant the killing of the express agents.

Feeling safe and satisfied with the letter, he was bold with adding on his address and where he could be found. That letter would fool any sheriff and stranger, he figured, and folding it up he stuck it in an envelope, sealed it and addressed it to Pete, after which he hid it under the marble top of a dresser in the room and there to stay until the first chance he got of mailing it. Maybe old Walters would be hitting for town most any time and visit with his daughter. He'd try and talk him into that in a roundabout way, and being that he, Tim, was on the job now, old Walters might just want to do that little thing if it was mentioned to him.

Tim felt a considerable better now that he'd decided to write the letter and had it ready to mail. He of course didn't see where it'd help him much, not if the killing was held against him, but he at least was showing good intentions, not that of a guilty man, and it might do some good in some way. If there was no killing against him, Pete would soon let him know and then he felt he could get clear pretty easy if all the money he got was returned. It would take his cash amount down quite a bit to make up the thousand he'd took out of the box but it would sure be worth it to be free. Now more than any time.

It had been hard at first for him to decide to turn the money back, for, like he'd thought right along, he didn't know if it would do him much good to do that. Then again he'd be broke and helpless to go on with what all he'd like to do. Another thing it would freshen the officers' minds about him in case they held the killing against him. That's what had held him back all this time, and what had decided him was the possibility that old Walters would be selling the ranch. He wanted that place for himself, and if he was free he figured he could somehow get it, and he'd then be able to enjoy it. Maybe he could run it on shares for old Walters, let the stud bunches and cattle increase as much as possible, get better prices, and with odd work such as running wild ones with Joshua or taking on some to break for others, he could in time manage to rake up enough to make a good payment on the place. Then with his freedom and Jane the rest would only be to his heart's content.

The more he thought on the subject the more he felt there was plenty to gain, and not much to lose only the money. He felt much relieved now that he'd decided to turn it back, like it was it that had been hanging over him and casting a shadow. How great he would feel now if all what he figured was against him was swept clean and he could start fresh, on this place, with Jane. Yep, that might be too much to hope for, but——

That evening, and now being anxious to get action, he came out in a roundabout way and suggested to old Walters that if there was any place he wanted to go or anything he wanted to do, like visiting his daughter for instance or any business he'd want to take care of in town, now would be a good time for him to go, while he had him to take care of the place and stock.

As Tim had figured, that came as a surprise to old Walters. He'd never thought of that, and now that he realized how free he was to come and go, feeling that all would be safe and well taken care of, he acted as tho he wanted wings.

"By Jaymeny Christmas, you know," he says all hilarious, "I've been alone and had to clamp down here so tight and for so long that going any place never come to me, just because I couldn't of went before if I wanted or should of. And lately I didn't know for sure how long you could be with me, so I didn't think of going. You're too valuable a man to waste your time staying here for long and I couldn't pay you the wages you're worth."

"Maybe we could work it on shares," Tim chips in, "and I'll make it your worth, at least as much as you're getting off the place now, not counting my share, and you wouldn't have to be living here if you didn't want to."

"Well, at that rate," says old Walters, thinking on the subject for a spell, "I wouldn't be in no hurry at all to sell the place, not as long as you wanted it. And I *would* like to go visit my daughter and take care of some business in town there which I been neglecting for a long time. Yes, Jerry, I sure would like to."

"Go right ahead," says Tim, grinning. "I'll be on the job here."

* * *

Tim went riding the next day, all pleased with himself and everything in general. He somehow felt that all would come out in a way where he'd soon be free of dodging and *live happily ever after*. He rode old Walters' range already with a feeling of ownership and he looked at the stock the same way. He'd soon be well enough now to work on the corrals and getting everything in shape. He'd start a garden too. He didn't know much about that only from when a kid at home and what he learned by being with Jane and her

Tim went riding the next day

mother. He did remember about planting flowers, and he'd get old Walters to get him a variety of seeds. That'd be light to pack.

While Tim rode, old Walters was busy as an old woman, getting a couple of old but good suits out, putting 'em in shape and gathering other things he wanted to take along. He'd decided to go in a buggy, for he could take more things with him that way and bring more back, whenever he would be back.

He run in a light team that day, a team that'd been ranging close and with his other broke stuff and unbroke geldings, then he mended the old harness, greased the buckboard, and with his town clothes packed up he was all set. He would be ready to start out at the break of day the next morning, figuring on making the sixty miles to town by sundown that day.

It was a cheerful supper for the two as Tim rode in that evening. He'd been riding one of old Walters' horses, and left Scorpion to a rest he didn't need. That horse was dozing by the corrals as he rode in, and Tim had to grin at the fat he was piling on, remarking that as a horse of Destiny he was sure getting out of shape.

Supper over with and all taken care of for a bright and early start in the morning, old Walters went out to set on the porch. Tim was already there and the two went on to enjoy the warm spring evening. There was no pinochle nor checkers played that evening, it had turned to conversation, about the stock, the ranch, of old Walters' going to town and Tim staying to hold down the place.

The conversation was going right along that way and agreeable when, as the evening shadows spread over the land, there come a sudden stop in the talk. Tim all at once went set and tense, and like a cougar spotting a hunter his gaze was fixed. Old Walters noticing his actions looked the direction Tim was but he couldn't see anything.

"What's wrong, son?" he finally asks, wondering.

"Just this," says Tim in a low voice. "Two riders are heading this way and they're not riding where they should." He pointed to a clump of cedars by the road leading into the ranch. "I got a glimpse of their hats on the other side of that clump there," he says, and he stood up.

"Well, what of it?" says old Walters, squinting at Tim. "We seen 'em first, didn't we?"

"Sure," grins Tim in a queer way. "But I'm bashful, and I don't want 'em to see me, none at all."

With that he went in the house, buckled on his six-shooter, pocketed the letter he'd wrote, and as he started for the corrals he just said to the wondering old timer: "You've never seen hide nor hair of such a feller as me in case they ask you. I'll be back soon as they're gone," and with that he went in a roundabout way to the corrals.

But he didn't know if he'd be back nor when, maybe never, and for the time he only wanted to saddle up Scorpion and get to rambling as quick as he could, for he had a strong hunch that one or both of them riders was packing a star. It was getting near dark, a good time to start out and make a lot of distance before morning come. He could be gone and on his way before the suspicious acting riders ever got to the house.

In the twilight of the day, which Tim was thankful for, he went to where Scorpion had been dozing when he rode in that evening. But the horse wasn't there now and nowheres close to the corrals. He could see the horses in the meadow, and going to them, figuring sure he'd be in the bunch, he was mighty surprised that he wasn't. All the horses was accounted for but him, and with a puzzled and worried look he started back for the corrals. Nothing was inside of them excepting one of old Walters' old pensioners which was used only to "jingle" on (wrangle).

Feeling kind of safe in the darkness that'd now come, Tim took his time more and went on looking for Scorpion. Maybe he'd got in the stable or chicken house and a door slammed shut on him. But the horse was in no such places, nor any other place where he'd be apt to be. More puzzled than ever and now fretting, Tim then made a circle of the whole meadow, from the edge of the canyon to the foot of the rim, and when he returned to the corrals once more he felt sure that that horse wasn't inside the fence nor around the ranch nowheres.

It was all a mystery as to how that horse could of disappeared so quick. Then, as Tim sort of rested on the edge of a manger in the dark stable and went on to thinking, it came to him that the two riders he'd seen might be responsible for the sudden disappearance of that horse. Maybe Scorpion had grazed out on the meadow and they'd run him off on him to be sure of leaving him afoot, knowing maybe that he wouldn't start out on any of old Walters' old horses.

Now he was in a predicament, he figured. There wasn't a horse around that was fit to ride out and expect to get any distance on. Then he thought of the team old Walters had run in that day, maybe one of them would do. But getting them in the corral would make sounds that could easy enough be heard from the house, and catching one and not knowing how that one would be to saddle and ride would be another thing, for a horse might be gentle in harness and at the same time be dynamite under the saddle.

He was sitting there in the dark and pondering on the subject when his thoughts was of a sudden jarred by a holler and he heard his name called. He recognized the voice as old Walters' and he wondered why he should be calling him, specially after being warned that there'd been no such a person as himself being seen anywhere any time. Maybe old Walters had got excited and forgot.

Tim went outside the stable and kneeling low he could see old Walters outlined against the sky. He was alone and still hollering as he came on towards the corrals. But Tim didn't budge nor answer, he only waited, wondering, and when old Walters come near he stood up and spoke low.

"What is it, Walt?" he says.

"A feller name of Pete something," says old Walters, glad to find Tim. "Claims to be an old friend of yours from the north and——"

Tim didn't wait to hear no more. He goosed old Walters in the ribs and started for the house at a fast gait, and looking thru the window inside the lighted house before he went in, making double sure that it was Pete a-standing by the stove there and rolling a smoke, he busted into the door and went on in to greet him.

Both was mighty glad to see one another, Tim the most surprised. He was going to jabber on and inquire how he come to find out where he was when Pete looked past him and winked, then Tim looked back, and standing behind the door with a sort of satisfied grin on his face he seen a plum stranger there.

Tim didn't have much chance to wonder before he heard Pete speak and say, "That's him, Sheriff."

At the sudden surprise and the word sheriff, Tim's mind went a-whirling. He looked back at Pete, all tense and on his toes, and like to ask him the meaning of the goings on. But he couldn't get nothing but a blank and grinning expression from that friend of his, and the stranger's, or sheriff's, face was the same.

The few seconds' stillness was finally broke by the sound of old Walters coming up on the porch, and wide eyed he entered the house, looking at one and then the other in turn. Then he just says, "What in the samhill?"

But what he said wasn't so much, it was the way

he *acted*, and quicker than anybody could see, or maybe he had it in his hand all the time, but anyhow Mr. Pete and the sheriff found themselves looking into the spouting end of a full grown .45, and "What in the samhill?" got to really mean something then.

Pete sizing up the situation was the first one to speak. "I'm done now, Sheriff," he says. "You do your duty, and better do it quick too before we both get it in the middle."

"You're durn tooting," hollers old Walters, all riled up. Then to Tim, he says, "Come on over here by me, son, and unlimber."

Tim moved a little and then turned to the still satisfied looking sheriff. "What's up?" he asks of him and then Pete. He felt that something queer was in the air, but not a trap.

"Better tell your pap to point his iron down," says the sheriff. "Then we'll talk."

"I'll leave that to him," answers Tim. "Go ahead and talk."

"All right," he went on, "and I'll say it quick because I usually feel sort of nervous when a gun is pointing my way. . . . The whole thing in a few words is that we've hunted high and low and finally located you thru the help of Pete here"—Tim squinted at the still grinning Pete—"only," he was hearing the sheriff say, "to compliment you in your part at capturing the bandits and to reward you for same."

It took a little while for that to sink in Tim's and old Walters' minds. The two looked at one another and blinked, and slowly, as it dawned on him, old Walters' gun begin to point down.

"Well, you goldurned jakanapes," he says, still half peeved. "Why in tarnation didn't you say so? You come near getting your fool hides turned into sieves, didn't you know that?"

"We know it now," says the sheriff, more at ease, "and it sure wasn't our idea of playing that we was going to make an arrest. That's too dangerous a kind of play, and it only turned out to look that way is all."

"Yes," Pete chips in. "We only wanted to make it a good surprise, and I guess we did. But knowing that you'd be on the lookout and ready to jump," he says to Tim, "we had to come in the way we did so you wouldn't fly the coop or start smoking us up on sight before you knew who we was and what we come for. So we had to go at it as tho we was on the trail of a sure enough outlaw and so we could get close to you first and have a chance to say a few words. But we didn't figure on running into a stack of fighting hornets like this or we'd sent a scout ahead with a white flag."

All understood now and the tenseness broke. Old Walters put his gun away to nobody knows where and went on with finishing the meal he'd started for the sheriff and Pete, happy again and wondering the while how come about the bandits and the reward. He would cook and listen, and then he would know.

"Well," says Pete to the sheriff, "I guess we're safe of 'our man' not running off with our horses now, so we better get 'em out of hiding and turn 'em on feed."

"Yeh," says Tim at that, "and Scorpion too."

"Scorpion?" says Pete, wondering. "Why, we didn't see him."

It was Tim's turn to wonder, and he didn't say anything about it. But as he went outside to show Pete and the sheriff where to put their horses for the night, he come near running smack bang into that horse, and now not over fifty yards from the corral. Scorpion had come out of his hiding place, and wherever that was, Tim couldn't begin to guess.

"Didn't want me to go, so you hid out on me, eh?" he says to the horse as he rubbed him on the nose. "Well," he went on after a spell, "that's a lot better than laying me flat so as to make me see. . . . And I guess now that old Joshua is right about you being a horse of Destiny. For without you and your kind of doings I'd been riding on long ago, still be on the dodge and hiding, and only half of me riding."

* * *

The gathering at old Walters' table that night was a cheerful one. Tim and Pete went on to talking of what all had happened since they'd last seen one another. They laughed now as Tim told how Scorpion had treated him, bunged him up as bad as he had Pete. "Yep," says Tim. "He treated me mighty rough all right, but I guess he had to so as to keep me where I was, and even if I did do a lot of fidgeting most of the time I'm sure glad for it now."

"Ycs," Pete agreed. "You'd of been riding on and playing lone wolf the rest of your life."

"Why didn't you write me as you said you would,

Didn't want me to go, so you hid out on me, eh?

you horsethief," Pete went on to ask, "and what's this new name the old gent here calls you?"

"Well," says Tim, "I didn't write because I was afraid somebody else would get to read the letter, and then I was planning on riding away to some other country all the time. As for the name it's not new, it's the one my dad and mother gave me, Jerry Nelson, and this is the only country I've ever used it in. I see now where I'm going to use it for good and right here on this ranch and range."

Old Walters and the sheriff kept an ear cocked to all of that as they, themselves, went on to talking of old times, politics and the country in general. Old Walters remembered the sheriff now, he'd helped elect him.

But as the talking went on, it soon come to the subject that was the most important right then, the subject of the hold up and which settled Tim's wondering as to his getting any reward when he'd felt right along he'd be lucky if he wasn't hung. It was some surprise to him and it took him a long time to realize all it meant. Yes, it took him days.

To begin with, and as the sheriff told the story, two of the bandits confessed of the robbery and killing, the other was convicted of another such a killing and the three was executed. The driver of the automobile was the only one to get off with his life, with a straight ninety-nine years of it to serve behind the bars.

It seemed like that gang had been a mighty tough one, maybe not so tough but crazy for thrills and notoriety, and they got more than all of that they wanted. But while they run loose they done plenty of harm and took some valuable lives, enough so that, all stacked up, there was close to $30,000 in reward put up for their capture. A mighty big reward, the biggest ever heard of, but nothing as compared to what it meant to have such kind caught up with and safe out of the way. What all they'd done and would of done if they could of gone on, if Tim hadn't jumped off the train after them as he did, made the big reward look only as a small tip.

"You could of collected all the reward as well as not," the sheriff says to him. "All you'd had to done was ride on in with 'em, and that would of been easy the way I heard how scared you had 'em, even if they'd found out there was only one of you."

"But what I can't figure out," Tim said to that, "is how I come in on any of the reward. I onlv run off with the money myself."

"Yes, but that money was a small matter as compared to what all the catching of that gang meant, what they'd done and was wanted for, train and bank robberies and killings galore. You took the guts and danger out of 'em and made 'em as harmless and easy to handle as so many dumb sheep. It would of been a very different story if they'd got off with the loot, had their artillery and all worked as they'd mapped out. They wouldn't of had a perforated gas tank then either, and went on full speed, all bloated with their glory and more cunning and fierce than ever.

"No, sir. If it was me that had any say you'd get two-thirds of that reward instead of only one-third. The people who reported 'em at the gasoline station are the ones who got the two-thirds, and they didn't do anything nor take any chances, only report, and any child can do that."

"But even at that, $10,000 is sure not to be snickered at for your share of the reward."

"Yeh, a doggone sight better than ten years in the pen," says Tim. "What I wanted most was to be clear and exonerated."

"You've got that," says the sheriff, "and a good reward to boot."

"That's sure fine, and I guess it'll take me a long time to realize it. . . . But I'm not so craving for the blood money, but then again, being I didn't set out to get it and that it ain't my fault it comes to me, I guess it'll be all right to take and use it. With the plans I have in mind now I can do that well. Yep, mighty well."

"And you're not the only one to get rewarded," the sheriff went on. "Pete, here, gets five thousand for digging up the money box, delivering it to the sheriff up north and then locating you here."

"But I don't want that five thousand," Pete chips in. "I was coming down thru this country anyhow. I'm on my way to Mexico; got a gold mine down there," he grinned, joking, "and I won't have no use for any such small amounts. Give it to Tim; if I'm guessing right I think he'll need it."

There was some discussing as to that for quite a spell, but finally and with threats from Tim that he wouldn't touch his reward unless Pete took his it all pacified down to where they'd both take their rewards and be happy about it. As a wind up and last resort, Pete went on to remark that he wasn't alone in the locating of Tim, that there was a lady in the case who was the most responsible and should have the reward. At that he unbuttoned a shirt pocket, pulled out a letter and handed it to Tim.

The sight of the handwriting was near enough for Tim to swallow his Adam's apple and guess the rest before he choked. It was Jane's, and as he read the letter he seen where she hid her purpose of writing in as good a way as he did in the letter he wrote himself, so Pete and nobody else would know the meaning.

Getting over his surprise, and wanting to hide his feeling he then dug up the letter he'd wrote, sealed, stamped and addressed and handed it to Pete and the sheriff for them to read, saying:

"Walt is going to town in the morning and I was going to have him mail this to you, Pete."

The letter was read carefully, even by old Walters, who leaned over Pete and finally said he couldn't make any sense of it. The sheriff added on that he couldn't of either if he didn't already know.

"I like the part about the sheep," finally grins Pete, who well understood the letter. "Maybe that's what'll become of you now."

"This is poor sheep country," says Tim, grinning back at him.

"But getting back on the subject now," says Pete, serious, "the lady who sent me the letter about returning the money and which led to finding you, Tim, is the one who is entitled to the reward."

"Yes," Tim says, sort of slow and absent minded-like. "But what I'd like to know is how she come to locate you. The most I remember ever mentioning was maybe your name, and as to your whereabouts only maybe the state."

"Well," Pete said, "that seemed to be aplenty for her. Look at the way the letter is addressed."

Tim picked up the envelope and looked and was puzzled some more. For the letter was addressed to the State Recorder of brands, to be forwarded to Mr. Pete Leon in care of the Cross Bell outfit in that state.

That was simple enough and, as Pete said, the letter was forwarded to the outfit's headquarters and was brought to him in good time by one of the riders from the wagon.

But what puzzled Tim was how come she got to know about the Cross Bell. He didn't recollect ever mentioning that iron to her. Then, as he thought on the subject, a grin of wonder begin to spread on his face. From the brand on Scorpion's hide is where she'd got it. She'd seen that it had been worked over and then had read the original. It took a sharp and knowing eye to do that, but she had such an eye, and Tim couldn't figure out of any other way she could of got to know of the brand, then she wrote to Pete thru the brand recorder.

"That's sure some detective work, I calls it," says Pete, as Tim told of his solution, and the sheriff and old Walters more than agreed to that.

"Sure is," says Tim. "But with all the credit that's

She'd seen that it had been worked over and then had read the original

due her I sure wouldn't mention no reward for what she done. That would only cheapen her sentiments and wouldn't at all do. I know the kind of reward she wants, the same as I do, and she'll share that with me. No more said on the subject, Pete, and that's understood, old boy."

Pete whistled in surprise at the serious way Tim spoke, and while fidgeting around for something to say the sheriff spoke up.

"If I might speak a little more on the subject," he says to Tim, "I would like to add on that Pete scraped up the thousand to even up the contents of the money that was originally in the box and so the check for the reward could be claimed." With that he reached in his jacket pocket, pulled out a wallet and dug out a certified check for nearly $10,000 and handed it to Tim, saying, "Not near as much as you had cached away, but you won't have to dodge to keep this." He handed Pete another such a check for five thousand, then he backed away from the table.

"You two fight it out between yourselves now," he says, all final, "I want to compliment you both on behalf of the state and I only wish there was many more like you boys. That's all, and best of luck."

Tim stared at his check, not like it was a check or that the amount meant anything to him, but like a precious release paper, a release from the shadow that'd been hanging and threatening over him and which had stood between him and all he'd wanted the most in the world.

Pete was the first to break the stillness. "Where do we go from here now, Tim?" he says.

Tim sort of shook himself, blinked at him and then answering only with a grin he got up from the table, hunted a pen and some ink, endorsed the check and handed it to old Walters, who took it, wondering.

"Take six thousand out of that for the ranch and stock," he says to him, "and put the rest in the bank for me, will you?" Then he slumped down in his chair, and grinning at the three around him, he added on, "I think I'll live."